STORIES
FROM
UNCLE REMUS

The Moon in the Mill Pond

STORIES

FROM

UNCLE REMUS

Adapted from the stories
by
Joel Chandler Harris

TIGER BOOKS INTERNATIONAL
LONDON

This edition published in 1994 by
Tiger Books International PLC, Twickenham, England.

© This edition Geddes & Grosset Ltd.

ISBN 1 85501 549 8

Printed in Slovenia.

CONTENTS

LIST OF ILLUSTRATIONS

I

UNCLE REMUS INITIATES THE LITTLE BOY

ONE EVENING recently, the lady whom Uncle Remus calls "Miss Sally" missed her little seven-year-old. Making search for him through the house and through the yard, she heard the sound of voices in the old man's cabin, and, looking through the window, saw the child sitting by Uncle Remus. His head rested against the old man's arm, and he was gazing with an expression of the most intense interest into the rough, weather-beaten face that beamed so kindly upon him. This is what Miss Sally heard:

"By and by, one day, after Brer Fox had been doing all that he could to catch Brer Rabbit, and Brer Rabbit had been doing all that he could to keep him from it, Brer Fox said to himself that he could play a trick upon Brer Rabbit, and he hadn't more than got the words out of his mouth when Brer Rabbit came bounding up the big road, looking just as plump, and as fat, and as saucy as a pig in a clover-field.

"'Hold on there, Brer Rabbit,' said Brer Fox.

"'I haven't time, Brer Fox,' said Brer Rabbit, putting on an extra spurt.

"'I want to have a talk with you, Brer Rabbit,' said Brer Fox.

"'All right, Brer Fox, but you had better shout from where you stand. I'm terribly full of fleas this morning,' said Brer Rabbit.

"'I saw Brer Bear yesterday,' said Brer Fox, 'and he was cross with me because you and I aren't good friends and don't live in a neighbourly way, so I told him that I would see you.'

"Then Brer Rabbit scratched one ear with his off hind-foot rather doubtfully, and he said:

"'Very well, Brer Fox. Suppose you drop around tomorrow and take dinner with me. We haven't got anything very grand at our house, but I expect the old woman and the children can manage to scramble around and get something for you to eat."

"'I'm agreeable, Brer Rabbit,' said Brer Fox.

"'Then I'll depend on you,' said Brer Rabbit.

"The next day Brer Rabbit and Mrs Rabbit got up early, before it was day, and raided a garden like Miss Sally's out there. They got some cabbages, and some Indian corn, and some 'sparrow-grass,' and made a fine dinner.

"Presently one of the little Rabbits, playing out in the backyard, came running in and shouting, 'Oh, Ma! Oh, Ma! I saw Mr Fox coming!' Then Brer Rabbit took the children by the ears and made them sit down, after which he and Mrs Rabbit dallied around waiting for Brer Fox. They kept on waiting, but no Brer Fox came. After a while Brer Rabbit went to the door softly and peeped out. There, sticking out from behind the corner, was the tip-end of Brer Fox's tail. Seeing this, Brer Rabbit shut the door and sat down. Then putting his paws behind his ears he began to sing:

> "'*The place whereabouts you spill the grease,*
> *Right there you are bound to slide,*
> *And where you find a bunch of hair,*
> *You'll surely find the hide.*'

"The next day Brer Fox sent word by Mr Mink, and excused himself because he was too poorly to come, and he asked Brer Rabbit to come and take dinner with him instead. Brer Rabbit said that he was agreeable.

"Presently, when the shadows were at their shortest, Brer Rabbit had a brush-up and sauntered down to Brer Fox's house. When he got there he heard somebody groaning, so he looked in at the door, and there he saw Brer Fox sitting up in a rocking-chair all wrapped up in flannel and looking very weak. Brer Rabbit looked all around, but he couldn't see any dinner. There was a big dish on the table and close by was a carving-knife.

"'It looks as if you are going to have chicken for dinner, Brer Fox,' said Brer Rabbit

"'Yes, Brer Rabbit, they are nice and fresh and tender,' said Brer Fox.

"Then Brer Rabbit pulled at his moustache and said:

"'You haven't any calamus root, have you, Brer Fox? I have got so that I can't eat chicken unless it is seasoned with calamus root.'

"With that Brer Rabbit leapt out of the door and, dodging among the bushes, sat there watching for Brer Fox. He didn't have to watch long either, because Brer Fox flung off the flannel and crept out of the house. Then he got where he could close in on Brer Rabbit, and presently Brer Rabbit shouted:

"'Oh, Brer Fox! I'll just put your calamus root on this stump. You had better come out and get it while it is fresh,' and with that Brer Rabbit galloped off home. Brer Fox hasn't caught him yet, and what is more, honey, he isn't going to catch him."

II

The Wonderful Tar-baby Story

IDN'T THE fox *ever* catch the rabbit, Uncle Remus?" asked the little boy the next evening.

"He came very near it, honey, as sure as you are born, Brer Fox did. One day after Brer Fox had fooled him with the calamus root, Brer Fox went to work and got some tar. This he mixed with some turpentine and fixed up an arrangement which he called a Tar-baby. He took this Tar-baby and put it in the big road, and he hid himself in the bushes so as to see what would happen. And he didn't have to wait very long, for soon Brer Rabbit came pacing down the road, *lippity-clippity, clippity-lippity*—just as saucy as a jay-bird. Brer Fox lay low. Brer Rabbit came prancing along until he spied the Tar-baby, and then he sat up on his hind-legs as if he were astonished. The Tar-baby, she stayed still, and Brer Fox, he lay low.

"'Good morning!' said Brer Rabbit—'nice weather this morning.'

"The Tar-baby said nothing, and Brer Fox, he lay low.

"'How do you feel this morning?' said Brer Rabbit.

"Brer Fox, he winked his eye slowly, and lay low, and the Tar-baby, she said nothing.

"'How are you then? Are you deaf?' said Brer Rabbit. 'Because if you are, I can shout louder,' said he.

"The Tar-baby stayed still, and Brer Fox, he lay low.

"'You are stuck up, that is what you are,' said Brer Rabbit, 'and I am going to cure you, that is what I am going to do,' said he.

"Brer Fox, he sort of chuckled in his stomach, he did, but the Tar-baby said nothing.

"'I am going to teach you how to talk to respectable folks, if it is the last act,' said Brer Rabbit. 'If you don't take off that hat and say, "How do you do?" I'm going to burst you wide open,' said he.

"The Tar-baby stayed still, and Brer Fox, he lay low.

"Brer Rabbit kept on asking him, and the Tar-baby, she kept on saying nothing, until presently Brer Rabbit drew back with his fist, he did, and *blip!* he struck her on the side of the head. And that was just where he made his mistake, for his fist stuck, and he couldn't pull it loose. The tar held him fast. But the Tar-baby, she stayed still, and Brer Fox, he lay low.

"'If you don't let me go, I'll knock you again,' said Brer Rabbit, and with that he gave her a blow with the other hand, and that stuck. The Tar-baby, she said nothing, and Brer Fox, he lay low.

"'Let me go, before I kick the very stuffing out of you,' said Brer Rabbit, but the Tar-baby, she said nothing. She just stayed there, and Brer Rabbit lost the use of one of his feet in the same way. Brer Fox, he lay low. Then Brer Rabbit cried out that if the Tar-baby didn't let him go he would butt her as the billy-goats do. And then he butted; so that his head was stuck. At that Brer Fox sauntered forward, looking just as innocent as a bird in a cage.

"'How do you do, Brer Rabbit?' said Brer Fox. 'You look rather stuck up this morning,' said he, and then he rolled on the ground, and laughed and laughed until he could laugh no more. 'I expect you will take dinner with me this time, Brer Rabbit. I have got some calamus root ready, and I am not going to take any excuse,' said Brer Fox."

Here Uncle Remus paused, and drew a two pound yam out of the ashes.

"Did the fox eat the rabbit?" asked the little boy to whom the story had been told.

"That's as far as the story goes," replied the old man. "He might have eaten him, and then again he might not have eaten him. Some say Judge Bear came along and set him free—some say that he didn't. I hear Miss Sally calling. You had better run along."

III

WHY BRER POSSUM LOVES PEACE

ONE NIGHT," said Uncle Remus, taking Miss Sally's little boy on his knee, and stroking the child's hair thoughtfully and caressingly, "one night Brer Possum called for Brer Coon, as they had arranged, and after gobbling up a dish of fried greens and smoking a cigar, they took a stroll to see how the rest of the settlement was getting along. Brer Coon, who always went very fast, raced along as if he had been Master John's bay pony, and Brer Possum, he went galloping too, so that they covered the ground in next to no time. Brer Possum had a good fill of date plums, and Brer Coon, he scooped up any amount of frogs and tadpoles. They ambled along in this way, just as agreeably as a basket of kittens, until by and by they heard Mr Dog talking to himself away off in the woods.

"'Suppose he attacks us, Brer Possum, what are you going to do?' said Brer Coon.

"Brer Possum gave a sort of laugh around the corners of his mouth. 'Oh, if he comes, Brer Coon, I am going to stand by you,' said Brer Possum. 'What are you going to do?' said he.

"'Who? Me?' said Brer Coon. 'If he attacks me, I warrant I'll give him one twist,' said he."

"Did the dog come?" asked the little boy.

"Go away, honey!" responded the old man in an impressive tone. "Get along! Mr Dog came, and that very soon. And he didn't wait to say 'How do you do?' either. He just sailed into the both of them. At the very first touch Brer Possum began to grin from ear to ear, and he rolled over as if he were dead. Then Mr Dog sailed into Brer Coon, and that is just where he made a great mistake, because Brer Coon was used to that sort of business, and he fairly wiped up the earth with him. You may well believe that when Mr Dog got a chance to make himself scarce he took it, and what there was left of him went skedaddling through the woods like a shot out of a musket. And Brer Coon licked himself into shape once more and went off too. As for Brer Possum, he lay there as if he were dead, until by and by he raised himself very carefully. Then, when he found that the coast was clear, he scrambled up and scampered off as if something was after him."

Here Uncle Remus paused long enough to pick up a live coal of fire in his fingers, transfer it to the palm of his hand, and thence to his clay pipe, which he had been filling—a proceeding that was viewed by the little boy with undisguised admiration. The old man then proceeded:

"The next time Brer Possum met Brer Coon, Brer Coon refused to answer when he said 'How do you do?' and this made Brer Possum feel very uncomfortable, seeing that they used to take so many trips together.

"'What makes you hold your head so high, Brer Coon?' said Brer Possum.

"'I am not having anything to do with cowards these days,' said Brer Coon. 'When I want you I'll send for you,' said he.

"That annoyed Brer Possum very much.

"'Who is a coward?' said he.

"'You are,' said Brer Coon, 'that is who. I am not having anything to do with those who lie down on the ground and pretend that they are dead when there is a free fight going on,' said he.

"Then Brer Possum laughed as if he would kill himself.

"'Why, Brer Coon, you don't think that I did that because I was afraid, do you?' said he. 'Why, I was no more afraid than you are at this minute. What was there to be afraid of?' said he. 'I knew you would beat Mr Dog if I didn't, and so I just lay there watching you shake him, and waiting to take part when the time came.'

"Brer Coon turned up his nose.

"'That's a very likely story,' said he. 'Why, Mr Dog had only just touched you when you rolled over, and lay there as if you were dead.'

"'That is what I was going to explain to you,' said Brer Possum. 'I was no more frightened than you are now, and I was just getting ready to give Mr Dog a sample of my jaw. But I'm the most ticklish fellow you ever saw, and no sooner did Mr Dog put his nose against my ribs than I began laughing, and I laughed until I lost all use of my limbs. It's a mercy for Mr Dog that I am ticklish, because otherwise I should surely have eaten him up. I don't mind fighting, Brer Coon, any more than you do, but I declare that I can't stand tickling. Give me a fight where no tickling is allowed, and I'm your man.'

"And to this very day," continued Uncle Remus, watching the smoke from his pipe curl upward over the little boy's head, "to this very day, Brer Possum is bound to surrender when you touch him in the short ribs, and he must laugh if he knows that he is going to be smashed for it."

IV

How Brer Rabbit was too sharp for Brer Fox

"UNCLE REMUS," said the little boy one evening, when he had found the old man with little or nothing to do, "did the fox kill and eat the rabbit when he caught him with the Tar-baby?"

"Dear me, honey, didn't I tell you about that?" replied the old man, chuckling slyly. "I certainly ought to have told you that, but old man Nod was riding on my eyelids, so that a little more and I should have forgotten my own name, and then here came your mammy calling for you.

"What did I tell you when I first began? I told you that Brer Rabbit was a very artful creature; at least that was what I meant to tell you. Well then, honey, don't you get any other idea in your head, because in those days Brer Rabbit and his family took the lead in any games that were going on, and nobody else could ever get the better of them. Before you wipe your eyes on account of Brer Rabbit, you wait and see exactly what happened to him. But that's neither here nor there.

"When Brer Fox found that Brer Rabbit was mixed up with the Tar-baby, he felt mighty pleased, and he rolled on the ground and laughed. By and by he got up and said:

"'Well, I expect I've got you this time, Brer Rabbit. Maybe I haven't, but I expect I have. You have been running round here and making fun of me for a very long time, but I think that you have come to the end of your tether. You have been playing your tricks and bouncing around in this neighbourhood until you have come to believe that you are the master of us all. And then you are always somewhere where you have no business to be. Who asked you to come and strike up an acquaintance with this Tar-baby? And who stuck you up where you are now? Nobody in the round world. You just stuck yourself on that Tar-baby without waiting to be invited, and there you are, and there you will stay while I make a pile of brushwood and set fire to it, for I am going to roast you whole this very day, for certain.'

"Then Brer Rabbit began to talk in a very humble tone of voice: 'I don't care what you do with me, Brer Fox, as long as you don't fling me in that brier-patch.'

"'It's so much trouble to kindle a fire,' said Brer Fox, 'that I expect I'll have to hang you.'

"'Hang me just as high as you please, Brer Fox,' said Brer Rabbit, 'but for the Lord's sake don't fling me in that brier-patch.'

"'I haven't got any string,' said Brer Fox, 'and now I expect I'll have to drown you.'

"'Drown me just as deep as you please, Brer Fox,' said Brer Rabbit, 'but, oh! don't fling me in that brier-patch.'

"'There isn't any water near,' said Brer Fox, 'and now I expect I'll have to skin you.'

"'Skin me, Brer Fox,' said Brer Rabbit, 'snatch out my eyeballs, tear out my ears by the roots, and cut off my legs,' said he, 'but please, Brer Fox, don't fling me in that brier-patch.'

"Of course Brer Fox wanted to hurt Brer Rabbit as much as he could, so he caught him by the hind-legs and slung him right in the middle of the brier-patch. There was a considerable flutter where Brer Rabbit struck the bushes, and Brer Fox hung around so as to see what would happen. By and by he heard some one calling him, and away up the hill he saw Brer Rabbit sitting crosslegged on a chestnut log, combing the pitch out of his fur with a chip. Then Brer Fox knew that he had been tricked very badly. Brer Rabbit could not help giving him some of his impudence, so he shouted:

"'Bred and born in a brier-patch, Brer Fox—bred and born in a brier-patch!' and with the same he skipped out just as merrily as a cricket on the hearth."

The Wonderful Tar-baby

Brer Fox invites Brer Rabbit to dinner

V

BRER RABBIT GROSSLY DECEIVES BRER FOX

THE LITTLE boy had not forgotten that the wicked fox was still in pursuit of the rabbit, and one evening he put his curiosity in the shape of a question:

"Uncle Remus, did the rabbit have to go clean away when he got loose from the Tar-baby?"

"Bless me, honey, that he didn't. Who? Him? You don't know anything at all about Brer Rabbit if that is what you think about him. Why should he go away? He might have kept out of the way until he had rubbed off the pitch from his fur, but it wasn't many days before he was running around the neighbourhood just the same as ever, and I am not sure if he wasn't more saucy than before.

"It seemed as if the story of how he got mixed up with the Tar-baby got round among the neighbours. At any rate Miss Meadows and the girls got wind of it, and the next time Brer Rabbit paid them a visit Miss Meadows tackled him about it, and the girls all began to giggle. Brer Rabbit sat up as cool as a cucumber and let them run on."

"Who was Miss Meadows, Uncle Remus?" inquired the little boy.

"Don't ask me, honey. She was in the story, and so were the girls, and I give you the story as it was given to me. Brer Rabbit sat there as quiet as a lamb, and then presently he crossed his legs, and slowly winked his eye, and said:

"'Ladies, Brer Fox was my daddy's riding-horse for thirty years; maybe more, but for thirty years that I know of.' Then he paid them his respects, touched his hat, and marched off, just as stiff and stuck up as a firestick.

"The next day Brer Fox paid a call, and when he began to laugh about Brer Rabbit, Miss Meadows and the girls told him what Brer Rabbit had said. Then Brer Fox ground his teeth sure enough, and he looked very crestfallen, but when he rose to go he said:

"'Ladies, I don't deny what you say, but I'll make Brer Rabbit eat his words here in front of you.' And with that off Brer Fox marched.

"When he got in the big road, he shook the dew off from his tail, and made straight for Brer Rabbit's house. When he got there, Brer Rabbit was expecting him, so that the door was shut fast. Brer Fox knocked. There was no answer. Brer Fox knocked again. No answer. Then he knocked a third time—*blam! blam!* Then Brer Rabbit cried in a very weak voice:

"'Is that you, Brer Fox? I want you to run for the doctor. That parsley which I ate this morning will be the death of me. Do, please, Brer Fox, run quick.'

"'I have come after you, Brer Rabbit,' said Brer Fox. 'There is going to be a party at Miss Meadows's. All the girls are there, and I promised that I would fetch you. The girls declared that it wouldn't be anything of a party unless you were there.'

"Then Brer Rabbit said that he was too ill, and Brer Fox said that he wasn't, and so they went at it hammer and tongs, disputing and contending. Brer Rabbit said that he couldn't walk. Brer Fox said that he would carry him. Brer Rabbit asked him how. Brer Fox said that he would carry him in his arms. Brer Rabbit said that he would drop him. Brer Fox declared that he wouldn't. Presently Brer Rabbit said he would go if Brer Fox would carry him on his back. Brer Fox said he would. Brer Rabbit then said that he couldn't ride without a saddle. Brer Fox said that he would get the saddle. Brer Rabbit said that he couldn't sit in the saddle unless he had a bridle to hold on by. Brer Fox said that he would get the bridle. Brer Rabbit said that he must have a bridle with blinkers, because Brer Fox would be shying at the stumps along the road, and fling him off. Brer Fox said that he would get a bridle with blinkers. At that Brer Rabbit said he would go. Then Brer

Fox said that he would ride Brer Rabbit nearly up to Miss Meadows's, and he could get down and walk the rest of the way. Brer Rabbit agreed, so Brer Fox set out to get the saddle and the bridle.

"Of course, Brer Rabbit knew the trick that Brer Fox was trying to play on him, and he determined to outdo him. By the time he had combed his hair and brushed his moustache and made himself generally smart, there came Brer Fox with saddle and bridle on, and looking as tricksy as a circus pony. He trotted up to the door and stood there pawing the ground and champing his bit just like a real horse. Brer Rabbit mounted, and off they went. Brer Fox couldn't see what was going on behind because of the blinkers, but presently he felt Brer Rabbit raise one of his feet.

"'What are you doing now, Brer Rabbit?' he asked.

"'Shortening the left stirrup, Brer Fox,' he said.

"By and by Brer Rabbit raised the other foot.

"'What are you doing now, Brer Rabbit?' he asked.

"'Pulling down my pants, Brer Fox,' said he.

"All the time, honey, would you believe it, Brer Rabbit was putting on his spurs, and when they got close to Miss Meadows's, where Brer Rabbit was to get off, Brer Fox made as if to stand still. Then Brer Rabbit clapped the spurs into Brer Fox's sides, and you can imagine how quickly he got over the ground. When they got up to the house, Miss Meadows and all the girls were sitting on the terrace, and instead of stopping at the gate, Brer Rabbit rode past, and then came galloping down the road and up to the stable where he hitched up Brer Fox. Then he sauntered into the house, shook hands with the girls, and sat there smoking his cigar just like a man from town. By and by he drew a long puff and let it out in a big cloud. Then he drew himself up and said:

"'Ladies, didn't I tell you that Brer Fox was the riding-horse for our family? He isn't so swift as he was, but I expect I can get him in condition in a month or so.'

"And then Brer Rabbit gave a grin, and the girls giggled. Miss Meadows praised the pony, and there was Brer Fox hitched fast to the horse-rack, unable to help himself."

"Is that all, Uncle Remus?" asked the little boy, as the old man paused.

"That isn't all, honey, but it won't do to give out too much cloth to cut out one pair of pants," replied the old man.

VI

BRER FOX IS AGAIN DECEIVED

WHEN MISS Sally's little boy went to Uncle Remus the next night to hear the conclusion of the adventure in which the rabbit made a riding-horse of the fox, to the great enjoyment and gratification of Miss Meadows and the girls, he found the old man in a bad humour.

"I'm not telling stories to bad children," said Uncle Remus curtly.

"But, Uncle Remus, I'm not bad," said the little boy plaintively.

"Who was that throwing stones at those chickens this morning? Who was that trying to knock out folk's eyes with a sling before dinner? Who was it that set the pointer puppy after my pig? Who was it that scattered my onion sets? Who was it that threw stones on the top of my house, so that one of them nearly came on my head?"

"Well, now, Uncle Remus, I didn't mean to do it. I won't do it any more. Please, Uncle Remus, if you will tell me, I'll run to the house and bring you some tea-cakes."

"Seeing them is better than hearing tell of them," replied the old man, the severity of his countenance relaxing somewhat; but the little boy darted out, and in a few minutes came running back with his pockets full and his hands full.

"I'll warrant your mammy will think that the rats' stomachs are getting bigger in this district when she comes to count up her cakes," said Uncle Remus, with a chuckle. "These," he continued, dividing the cakes into two equal parts—"these I'll tackle now, and these I'll put by for Sunday.

"Let me see. I almost forget whereabouts Brer Fox and Brer Rabbit were."

"The rabbit rode the fox to Miss Meadows's, and hitched him to the horse-rack," said the little boy.

"Why, of course he did," said Uncle Remus. "Of course he did. Well, Brer Rabbit rode Brer Fox, and tied him to the rack, and then sat out on the veranda with the girls smoking his cigar as proudly as possible. The girls talked, they sang, and they played the piano, until the time came for Brer Rabbit to be going. He wished them all goodbye, and strutted out to the horse-rack just as if he were the chief of the policemen. Then he mounted Brer Fox and rode off.

"Brer Fox didn't say anything at all. He just flew along and kept his mouth shut. Brer Rabbit knew that there was trouble in store for him and he felt very frightened. Brer Fox trotted on until he got in the long lane, out of sight of Miss Meadows's house, and then he let himself go. He ripped and he reared; he fumed and he glared; he snorted and he cavorted."

"What was he doing that for, Uncle Remus?" the little boy inquired.

"He was trying to fling Brer Rabbit off his back, to be sure. But he might just as well have tried to wrestle with his own shadow. Every time that he humped himself Brer Rabbit clapped the spurs in him, and so they had it up and down. Brer Fox fairly tore up the ground, and he jumped so high and he jumped so quickly that he very nearly snatched off his own tail. They kept on in this way until Brer Fox lay down and rolled over. This rather unsettled Brer Rabbit, but by the time Brer Fox got on his feet again, Brer Rabbit was going through the bushes as fast as any race-horse. Brer Fox set out after him, and he ran him so close that it was as much as Brer Rabbit could do to get in a hollow tree. The hole was too small for Brer Fox, so he had to lie down and rest and collect his wits.

"While he was lying there, Mr Buzzard came flying along, and seeing Brer Fox stretched out on the ground, he alighted and had a good look. Then Mr Buzzard gave his wings a shake, and putting his head on one side, said to himself:

"'Brer Fox is dead, and I am so sorry.'

"'No, I am not dead neither,' said Brer Fox. 'I've got old man Rabbit shut up in here, and I'm going to get him this time if it takes me till Christmas.'

"Then after some more talk Brer Fox struck a bargain that Mr Buzzard was to watch the hole and keep Brer Rabbit there while Brer Fox went after his axe. Then Brer Fox cantered off, and Mr Buzzard took his stand at the hole. By and by, when all was still, Brer Rabbit scrambled down close to the hole, and shouted:

"'Brer Fox! Oh! Brer Fox!'

"Brer Fox was gone, and nobody said anything. Then Brer Rabbit cried out as if he was mad:

"'You needn't speak unless you want to. I know you are there and I don't care. I only wanted to tell you how I do wish that Brer Buzzard was here.'

"Then Mr Buzzard tried to talk like Brer Fox:

"'What do you want with Mr Buzzard?' said he.

"'Oh, nothing in particular, except that there is the fattest grey squirrel here that I ever saw, and if Brer Buzzard was anywhere near he would be glad indeed to get him.'

"'How is Mr Buzzard going to get him?' said the Buzzard.

"'Well, there's a little hole on the other side of the tree,' said Brer Rabbit, 'and if Brer Buzzard were here so that he could take up his stand there, I would drive that squirrel out.'

"'Drive him out then,' said Mr Buzzard, 'and I'll see that Brer Buzzard gets him.'

"Then Brer Rabbit made a great racket, as if he were driving something out, and Mr Buzzard rushed round to catch the squirrel. As soon as he did so Brer Rabbit dashed out and flew for home."

At this point Uncle Remus took one of the tea-cakes, held his head back, opened his mouth, dropped the cake in with a sudden motion, and looked at the little boy with an expression of astonishment. Then he closed his eyes and began to chew, mumbling as an accompaniment the plaintive tune of *Don't you Grieve after Me.*

The meeting was over; but, before the little boy went into the 'big house,' Uncle Remus laid his rough hand tenderly on the child's shoulder, and remarked in a confidential tone:

"Honey, you must get up early on Christmas morning and open the door, because I am going to bounce in on Master John and Miss Sally, and ask for a Christmas box as I used to before the war when the old mistress was alive. I'll be bound they won't forget this old man, either. When you hear me calling the pigs, honey, you just get up and unfasten the door. I warrant I'll give Master John a surprise."

VII

BRER FOX IS OUTDONE BY BRER BUZZARD

I F I AM not making any mistake," remarked Uncle Remus, as the little boy came tripping in to see him after supper, "Mr Buzzard was guarding the hollow where Brer Rabbit went in, and where he came out."

The silence of the little boy verified the old man's recollection.

"Well, Mr Buzzard felt very, very lonely, but he had promised Brer Fox that he would stay, and he made up his mind that he would remain there and join in the joke. And he didn't have to wait long, either, because presently there came Brer Fox galloping through the woods with his axe on his shoulder.

"'How do you think Brer Rabbit is getting on, Brer Buzzard?' said Brer Fox.

"'Oh, he is in there,' said Brer Buzzard. 'He is remarkably still, though. I expect he is taking a nap.'

"'Then I'm just in time to wake him up,' said Brer Fox. And with that he flung off his coat, and spit on his hands, and grabbed the axe. Then he drew back and came down on the tree—*pow!* And every time that he came down with his axe—*pow!*—Mr Buzzard he stepped high and cried:

"'Oh, he is in there, Brer Fox. He is in there, right enough.'

"And every time that a chip would fly off, Mr Buzzard would jump and dodge and put his head on one side, shouting:

"'He is in there, Brer Fox. I heard him. He is in there right enough.'

"And Brer Fox banged away at that hollow tree, like a man splitting rails. Presently, after he had almost cut through the tree, he stopped so as to catch his breath, and saw Mr Buzzard laughing behind his back. Then and there, without going any further, Brer Fox smelt a rat. But Mr Buzzard kept on shouting:

"'He is in there, Brer Fox. He is in there right enough. I saw him.'

"Then Brer Fox pretended to peep into the hollow, and he said:

"'Come here, Brer Buzzard, and see if this isn't Brer Rabbit's foot hanging down.'

"And Mr Buzzard came stepping up, just as if he were treading on thorns, and stuck his head in the hole. No sooner had he done that than Brer Fox grabbed him. Mr Buzzard flapped his wings, and wriggled round smartly enough, but it was of no use. Brer Fox had the advantage of the grip, and he held him close to the ground. Then Mr Buzzard cried at the top of his voice:

"'Let me alone, Brer Fox. Turn me loose,' said he; 'Brer Rabbit will get out. You are getting close to him, and eleven more blows will reach him.'

"'I'm nearer to you, Brer Buzzard,' said Brer Fox, 'than I shall ever be to Brer Rabbit this day. Why did you make a fool of me?'

"'Let me alone, Brer Fox,' said Mr Buzzard, 'my old woman is waiting for me. Brer Rabbit is in there.'

"'There is a bunch of his fur on that blackberry bush,' said Brer Fox, 'and that isn't the way he came.'

"Then Mr Buzzard told Brer Fox exactly how it was, and he declared that Brer Rabbit was the meanest creature that he had ever met. Then Brer Fox said:

"'That's neither here nor there, Brer Buzzard. I left you here to watch this hole, and I left Brer Rabbit inside. I come back and I find you at the hole and Brer Rabbit isn't inside. I am going to make you pay for it. I have been made such a fool of that even a beetle will sit on a log and laugh at me. I am going to fling you on a heap of brushwood and burn you up.'

"'If you fling me on the fire, Brer Fox, I shall fly away.'

"'Well then, I'll settle your affair at once,' said Brer Fox, and with that he seized Mr Buzzard by the tail and made as if to dash him against the ground, but just at that time the tail feathers came out, and Mr Buzzard sailed off like a balloon. As he rose, he answered:

"'You give me a good start, Brer Fox,' and Brer Fox sat there and watched him fly out of sight."

"But what became of the rabbit, Uncle Remus?" asked the little boy.

"Don't you bother about Brer Rabbit, honey; don't worry yourself about him. You heard where he went in and how he came out. This cold snap eats into my very bones," continued the old man, putting on his hat and picking up his walking-stick. "It shrivels me up, and I must look round and see if I can find some Christmas leavings."

VIII

Brer Tarrypin appears upon the Scene

iss Sally's little boy again occupying the anxious position of auditor, Uncle Remus took the shovel and "put the noses of the chunks together," as he expressed it, and then began:

"One day Brer Rabbit declared that he was going to drop in and see Miss Meadows and the girls, so he got out his piece of looking-glass, smartened himself up, and set out. Going cantering along the road, who should Brer Rabbit run up against but old Brer Tarrypin—the same old one-and-sixpence. Brer Rabbit stopped and rapped on the roof of Brer Tarrypin's house."

"On the roof of his house, Uncle Remus?" interrupted the little boy.

"Of course, honey, Brer Tarrypin carries his house with him. Rain or shine, hot or cold, strike up with old Brer Tarrypin when you will and while you may, and wherever you find him you will find his house. It is just as I tell you. So then! Brer Rabbit rapped on the roof of Brer Tarrypin's house, and asked him whether he was in. Brer Tarrypin said that he was, and then Brer Rabbit said, 'How do you do?' and Brer Tarrypin answered, 'How do you do?' Then Brer Rabbit asked where Brer Tarrypin was going, and Brer Tarrypin said that he wasn't going anywhere in particular. With that Brer Rabbit declared that he was on his way to see Miss Meadows and the girls, and he asked Brer Tarrypin if he wouldn't go along with him. Brer Tarrypin responded that he didn't care if he did, and so they set out together. They had plenty of time to talk along the way, but by and by they got there. Miss Meadows and the girls came to the door and asked them in, so in they went.

"When they got in, Brer Tarrypin was so flat-footed that he was too low on the floor, and he wasn't high enough in a chair. But while they were all scrambling around trying to get Brer Tarrypin a chair, Brer Rabbit picked him up and put him on the shelf by the water-bucket, and there Brer Tarrypin lay back, just as proud as any man with a cooked 'possum.

"Of course, the talk fell on Brer Fox, and Miss Meadows and the girls made a great fuss about what a wonderful riding-horse Brer Fox was, and they poked fun, and laughed and giggled just as girls do in these days. Brer Rabbit sat there in his chair smoking his cigar. Then he cleared his throat, and said:

"'I would have ridden him over this morning, ladies, but I rode him so hard yesterday that he went lame in the off foreleg, and I expect that I shall have to get rid of him.'

"Then Brer Tarrypin said:

"'Well, if you are going to sell him, Brer Rabbit, sell him somewhere out of this neighbourhood, because he has been here much too long. Only the day before yesterday Brer Fox passed me on the road, and what do you think he said?'

"'Dear me, Brer Tarrypin,' said Miss Meadows, 'you don't mean to say that he used bad words?' and then the girls held their fans before their faces.

"'Oh, no, ma'am,' said Brer Tarrypin, 'he didn't use bad words, but he shouted, "Heyo, Stinking Jim!"'

"'Oh, my! you hear that, girls?' said Miss Meadows; 'Brer Fox called Brer Tarrypin "Stinking Jim,"' and then Miss Meadows and the girls all said that they were surprised that Brer Fox could talk like that about a nice man like Brer Tarrypin.

"But goodness me, honey! while all this was going on, Brer Fox was standing at the back door with one ear at the cat-hole listening. Eavesdroppers never hear any good of themselves, and the way Brer Fox was abused that day was a caution.

"Presently Brer Fox put his head in at the door and shouted:

"'Good evening, folks, I wish you well,' and with that he made a dash for Brer Rabbit. Miss Meadows and the girls cried and shrieked, and Brer Tarrypin scrambled round on his shelf until off he tumbled, and *blip!* he struck Brer Fox on the back of his head. This stunned Brer Fox, and when he gathered his wits together again, all he saw was a pot of greens turned over in the fireplace, and a broken chair. Brer Rabbit was gone, and Brer Tarrypin was gone, and Miss Meadows and the girls were gone."

"Where did the rabbit go, Uncle Remus?" the little boy asked, after a pause.

"Bless your soul, honey! Brer Rabbit cleared up the chimney, that was what turned the pot of greens over. Brer Tarrypin crept under the bed, and got behind the clothes-chest, and Miss Meadows and the girls ran out into the yard.

"Brer Fox looked round and felt the back of his head, where Brer Tarrypin struck him, but he saw no sign of Brer Rabbit. But the smoke of the fire going up the chimney got the better of Brer Rabbit, and presently he sneezed—*huckychow!*

"'Aha!' said Brer Fox. 'You are there, are you? Well, I am going to smoke you out, if it takes a month. You are mine this time.'

"Brer Rabbit said nothing.

"'Aren't you coming down?' said Brer Fox.

"Brer Rabbit said nothing. Then Brer Fox went out after some wood, and when he came back he heard Brer Rabbit laughing.

"'What are you laughing at, Brer Rabbit?' said Brer Fox.

"'I can't tell you, Brer Fox,' said Brer Rabbit.

"'You had better tell, Brer Rabbit,' said Brer Fox.

"'It's nothing but a box of money that somebody has gone and left here in the chink of the chimney,' said Brer Rabbit.

"'I don't believe you,' said Brer Fox.

"'Look up and see,' said Brer Rabbit, and when Brer Fox looked up Brer Rabbit spit tobacco-juice right in his eyes, so that Brer Fox had to run out to the stream to wash it out. Then Brer Rabbit came down and wished the ladies goodbye.

"'How did you get rid of him, Brer Rabbit?' said Miss Meadows.

"'Who? Me?' said Brer Rabbit. 'Why, I only told him that if he didn't go home and stop playing pranks on respectable folks that I would take him out and thrash him.'"

"And what became of the terrapin?" asked the little boy.

"Oh, now then!" exclaimed the old man, "children can't expect to know all about everything before they get some rest. Those eyelids of yours want to be propped up with straws this minute."

IX

BRER WOLF MAKES A MISTAKE

"I BELIEVE THAT your ma has company," said Uncle Remus, as the little boy entered the old man's door with a huge piece of mince-pie in his hand, "and if she hasn't got company, then she has dropped the cupboard key somewhere and you have found it."

"Well, I just saw the pie lying there, Uncle Remus, and I thought I would fetch it out to you."

"To be sure, honey," replied the old man, regarding the child with admiration. "To be sure, honey, that alters matters. Christmas things are out of date, and they have no business to be lying around loose. This pie," Uncle Remus continued, holding it up and measuring it with an experienced eye, "will give me strength to follow after Brer Fox and Brer Rabbit and the other creatures that they had with them."

Here the old man paused and proceeded to demolish the pie—a feat accomplished in a very short time. Then he wiped the crumbs from his beard and began:

"Brer Fox felt so bad, and he got so mad about Brer Rabbit, that he didn't know what to do, and he looked mighty downhearted. By and by, one day while he was going along the road, old Brer Wolf came up with him. When they had finished saying 'How do you do?' and asking after one another's family connexions, Brer Wolf declared that there must be something wrong with Brer Fox. Brer Fox declared that there wasn't, and he went on and laughed and made a great to-do because Brer Wolf looked as if he had a suspicion of something or other. But Brer Wolf had a very long head and he broached the subject of

Brer Fox tackles Brer Tarrypin

Brer Rabbit's carryings-on, because the way that Brer Rabbit had deceived Brer Fox had got to be the talk of the neighbourhood. Then Brer Fox and Brer Wolf chatted away, until presently Brer Wolf up and said that he had made a plan by which they could trap Brer Rabbit. Brer Fox asked how it was to be done. Brer Wolf told him that the way to catch Brer Rabbit was to get him to go in Brer Fox's house. Brer Fox knew Brer Rabbit of old, and he knew that that sort of game was played out, but Brer Wolf talked in a very persuasive way.

"'How are you going to get him in there?' said Brer Fox.

"'Fool him in there,' said Brer Wolf.

"'Who is going to do the fooling?' said Brer Fox.

"'I'll do the fooling,' said Brer Wolf, 'if you will do the gaming.'

"'How are you going to do it?' said Brer Fox.

"'You run along home, and lie on the bed as if you are dead, and don't you say anything until Brer Rabbit comes and puts his hands on you,' says Brer Wolf, 'and if we don't get him for supper, then Joe's dead and Sal's a widow.'

"This looked like a very fine-game, so Brer Fox agreed, and ambled home while Brer Wolf marched off to Brer Rabbit's house. When he got there, it looked as if nobody were at home, but Brer Wolf walked up and knocked at the door—*blam! blam!* Nobody came. Then he let loose and knocked again—*blim! blim!*

"'Who is there?' said Brer Rabbit.

"'A friend,' said Brer Wolf.

"'Too many friends spoil the dinner,' said Brer Rabbit. 'Which one is this?'

"'I bring bad news, Brer Rabbit,' said Brer Wolf.

"'Bad news is soon told,' said Brer Rabbit.

"By this time Brer Rabbit had come to the door with his head tied in a red handkerchief.

"'Brer Fox died this morning,' said Brer Wolf.

"'Where's your mourning gown, Brer Wolf?' said Brer Rabbit.

"'I am going after it now,' said Brer Wolf. 'I just called to let you know the news. I went down to Brer Fox's house a little while ago, and there I found him stiff.'

"Then Brer Wolf trotted off. Brer Rabbit sat down and scratched his head. Presently he said to himself that he believed he would drop around by Brer Fox's house so as to see how the land lay. No sooner said than done. Up he jumped and out he went. When Brer Rabbit got close to Brer Fox's house, all looked lonesome. Then he went nearer. Nobody was stirring, so he looked in, and there lay Brer Fox stretched out on the bed as big as life. Then Brer Rabbit talked to himself.

"'Nobody round here to look after Brer Fox—not even Brer Buzzard come to the funeral. I hope Brer Fox isn't dead, but I expect he is. Even Brer Wolf has gone and left him. It's the busy season with me, but I'll sit up with him. He seems as if he is dead, yet he may not be,' said Brer Rabbit. 'When a man goes to see dead folks, dead folks always raise their hind-leg and shout, "*Wahoo!*"'

"Brer Fox stayed still. Then Brer Rabbit talked a little louder:

"'This is mighty funny. Brer Fox looks as if he is dead, yet he doesn't act as if he is dead. Dead folks hoists their hind-leg and shouts "*Wahoo!*" when a man comes to see them,' said Brer Rabbit.

"Sure enough, Brer Fox lifted up his foot and shouted '*Wahoo!*' and Brer Rabbit tore out of the house as if the dogs were after him. Brer Wolf was mighty smart, but the next time you hear about him, honey, he'll be in trouble. You just hold your breath and wait."

X

BRER FOX TACKLES BRER TARRYPIN

ONE DAY," said Uncle Remus, sharpening his knife on the palm of his hand—"one day Brer Fox struck up with Brer Tarrypin right in the middle of the big road. Brer Tarrypin had heard him coming, and he made up his mind that he would keep one eye open; but Brer Fox was most polite, and he opened the conversation as if he hadn't seen Brer Tarrypin since the last flood.

"'Heyo, Brer Tarrypin, where have you been all this time?' said Brer Fox.

"'Lounging around, Brer Fox, lounging around,' said Brer Tarrypin.

"'You don't look so spruce as you did, Brer Tarrypin,' said Brer Fox.

"'Lounging around and suffering,' said Brer Tarrypin again.

"Then the talk went on in this way:

"'What is the matter with you, Brer Tarrypin? Your eye looks very red,' said Brer Fox.

"'Goodness me, Brer Fox, you don't know what trouble is. You haven't been lounging around and suffering,' said Brer Tarrypin.

"'Both eyes are red, and you look as if you are very weak, Brer Tarrypin,' said Brer Fox.

"'Goodness me, Brer Fox, you don't know what trouble is,' said Brer Tarrypin.

"'What is the matter with you now, Brer Tarrypin?' said Brer Fox.

"'I took a walk the other day, and a man came along and set the field afire. Goodness me, you don't know what trouble is,' said Brer Tarrypin.

"'How did you get out of the fire, Brer Tarrypin?' said Brer Fox.

"'I sat and bore it, Brer Fox,' said Brer Tarrypin. 'I sat and bore it, but the smoke got in my eye, and the fire scorched my back,' said Brer Tarrypin.

"'And it also burnt your tail off,' said Brer Fox.

"'Oh, no, there's the tail, Brer Fox,' said Brer Tarrypin, and with that he uncurled his tail from underneath his shell. No sooner did he do that than Brer Fox seized it and shouted:

"'Oh, yes, Brer Tarrypin! Oh, yes! And so you are the man who struck me on the head at Miss Meadows's, are you? You are in with Brer Rabbit, are you? Well, I'm going to do for you.'

"Brer Tarrypin begged and begged, but it wasn't any use. Brer Fox had been fooled so often that he was determined to finish Brer Tarrypin. Then Brer Tarrypin begged Brer Fox not to drown him, but Brer Fox couldn't promise. Then he begged Brer Fox to burn him because he was used to fire, but Brer Fox wouldn't say anything. Presently Brer Fox dragged Brer Tarrypin off a little way below the spring-house, and soused him in the water. Then Brer Tarrypin began to cry out:

"'Let go that root and catch hold of me. Let go that root and catch hold of me.'

"Brer Fox shouted back:

"'I haven't got hold of any root, and I have got hold of you.'

"Brer Tarrypin kept on crying:

"'Catch hold of me I'm drowning—let go that root and hold me.'

"Sure enough, Brer Fox let go his tail, and Brer Tarrypin went down to the bottom—*kerblunkity-blink!*"

Uncle Remus said this in a way so peculiar that the little boy asked:

"How did he go to the bottom, Uncle Remus?"

"*Kerblunkity-blink!*"

"Was he drowned, Uncle Remus?"

"Who? Old man Tarrypin? Are you drowned when your mother tucks you up in bed?"

"Well, no," said the little boy doubtfully.

"Old man Tarrypin was at home, I tell you, honey. *Kerblinkity-blink!*"

XI

The Awful Fate of Brer Wolf

UNCLE REMUS was half-soling one of his shoes, and Miss Sally's little boy had been handling his awls, his hammers, and his knives to such an extent that the old man was compelled to assume a threatening attitude; but peace reigned again, and the little boy perched himself on a chair, watching Uncle Remus driving in pegs.

"Folks who are always pestering people, and interfering with what isn't theirs, never come to a good end. There was Brer Wolf; instead of minding his own business, he must go in partnership with Brer Fox, and there was scarcely a minute in the day but what he was after Brer Rabbit. He kept on and kept on, until the first news you heard was that he was caught—and he was caught very badly."

"Goodness, Uncle Remus! I thought the wolf let the rabbit alone after he had tried to fool him about the fox being dead."

"Better let me tell this my way. By and by it will be your bedtime, and Miss Sally will be calling for you. Then you will be whimpering round, and Master John will bring up the rear with that strap which I made for him."

The child laughed, and playfully shook his fist in the simple, serious face of the venerable old man, but said no more. Uncle Remus waited awhile to be sure that there was to be no other demonstration, and then proceeded:

"Brer Rabbit didn't have any peace whatever. He couldn't leave home unless Brer Wolf would make a raid, and carry off some of the family. Brer Rabbit built himself a straw house, and that was torn down. Then he made a house with pinetops, and that went the same way. Then he made himself a bark house, and that was raided, and every time that he lost a house he lost one of his children. At last Brer Rabbit got mad, and used very strong language. More than that, he went off and got some carpenters, and they built him a plank house with rock foundations. After that he was able to have some peace and quietness. He could go out and pass the time of day with his neighbours, and come back and sit by the fire, and smoke his pipe and read his newspaper, just like any other man who has a family. He made a hole in the cellar where the little Rabbits could hide when there was a great disturbance in the neighbourhood, and the latch of the front door worked on the inside. Brer Wolf saw how the land lay, and he lay low. The little Rabbits were very frightened, but cold chills no longer ran up Brer Rabbit's back when he heard Brer Wolf go galloping by.

"By and by, one day when Brer Rabbit was arranging to call on Miss Coon, he heard a tremendous stir and clatter up the big road, and almost before he could prick up his ears to listen, Brer Wolf ran in the door. The little Rabbits went into their hole in the cellar, as quickly as you could blow out a candle. Brer Wolf was all covered in mud, and very nearly winded.

"'Oh, do pray save me, Brer Rabbit!' said Brer Wolf. 'Do please, Brer Rabbit! The dogs are after me and they will tear me up. Don't you hear them coming? Oh, do please save me, Brer Rabbit! Hide me somewhere where the dogs won't get me.'

"No quicker said than done.

"'Jump in that big chest, Brer Wolf,' said Brer Rabbit; 'jump in there and make yourself at home.'

"In jumped Brer Wolf, and down came the lid. Into the hasp went the hook, and there Mr Wolf was.

"Then Brer Rabbit went to the looking-glass, and winked at himself. After that he drew the rocking-chair in front of the fire, and took a big chew of tobacco."

"Tobacco, Uncle Remus?" asked the little boy incredulously.

"Rabbit tobacco, honey. You know the plant that Miss Sally puts among the clothes in the trunk; well, that is rabbit tobacco. Then Brer Rabbit sat there a long time, turning his mind over, and working his thinking machine. Presently he got up, and began to bustle around. Then Brer Wolf said:

"'Are the dogs all gone, Brer Rabbit?'

"'I fancy I heard one of them smelling around the chimney-corner just now.'

"Then Brer Rabbit got the kettle and filled it full of water and put it in the fire.

"'What are you doing now, Brer Rabbit?'

"'I'm arranging to make you a nice cup of tea, Brer Wolf.'

"Then Brer Rabbit went to the cupboard and got the gimlet, and commenced to bore little holes in the lid of the chest.

"'What are you doing now, Brer Rabbit?'

"'I'm boring little holes so that you will be able to breathe, Brer Wolf.'

"Then Brer Rabbit went out and got some more wood, and flung it on the fire.

"'What are you doing now, Brer Rabbit?'

"'I'm making up the fire so that you won't get cold, Brer Wolf.'

"Then Brer Rabbit went down into the cellar, and fetched out all his children.

"'What are you doing now, Brer Rabbit?'

"'I'm telling my children what a nice man you are, Brer Wolf.'

"And the children had to put their hands before their mouths to keep from laughing. Then Brer Rabbit got the kettle and began to pour the hot water on the lid of the chest.

"'What is that I hear, Brer Rabbit?'

"'You hear the wind blowing, Brer Wolf'

"Then the water began to soak through.

"'What is that I feel, Brer Rabbit?'

"'You feel the fleas biting, Brer Wolf'

"'They are biting very hard, Brer Rabbit'

"'Turn over on the other side, Brer Wolf'

"'What is that I feel now, Brer Rabbit?'

"'Still you feel the fleas, Brer Wolf'

"'They are eating me up, Brer Rabbit'

"And those were the last words of Brer Wolf, because the scalding water did the business.

"Then Brer Rabbit called in his neighbours, and they held a regular jubilee. And if you go to Brer Rabbit's house now, I don't know but what you will find Brer Wolf's hide hanging in the back porch, all because he was so busy with other folks' affairs."

XII

BRER FOX AND THE DECEITFUL TOADS

HEN THE little boy ran in to see Uncle Remus the night after he had told him of the awful fate of Brer Wolf, the only response to his greeting was:

"I-doom-er-ker-kum-mer-ker!"

No explanation could convey an adequate idea of the intonation and pronunciation which Uncle Remus brought to bear upon this wonderful word. Those who can recall to mind the peculiar gurgling, jerking, liquid sound made by pouring water from a large jug, or the sound produced by throwing several stones in rapid succession into a pond of deep water, may be able to form a very faint idea of the sound, but it cannot be reproduced in print. The little boy was astonished.

"What did you say, Uncle Remus?"

"I-doom-er-ker-kum-mer-ker! I-doom-er-ker-kum-mer-ker!"

"What is that?"

"That is Tarrypin's talk, that is. Bless your heart, honey," continued the old man, brightening up, "when you are as old as I am—when you see what I see, and hear what I hear, the creatures that you can't talk with will be very few—they will that. Why, there is an old grey rat that comes around here, and time after time he comes out when you are all gone to bed and sits there in the corner and dozes, and we talk by the hour. What that old rat doesn't know isn't in the spelling-book. Just now, when you ran in and interrupted me, I was going over in my mind what Brer Tarrypin said to Brer Fox when he turned him loose in the stream."

"What did he say, Uncle Remus?"

"That is what he said—'I-doom-er-ker-kummer-ker!' Brer Tarrypin was at the bottom of the pond, and he talked back in bubbles—'I-doom-er-ker-kum-mer-ker!' Brer Fox didn't say anything, but Brer Bullfrog, who was sitting on the bank, heard Brer Tarrypin, and he answered:

"'Jug-e-rum-kum-dum! Jug-er-rum-kum-dum!'

"Then another Frog said:

"'Knee-deep! Knee-deep!'

"Then old Brer Bullfrog shouted:

"'Don't-you-believe-him! Don't-you-believe-him!'

"Then the bubbles came up from Brer Tarrypin:

"'I-doom-er-ker-kum-mer-ker!'

"Then another Frog sang out:

"'Wade in! Wade in!'

"Then old Brer Bullfrog talked in his hoarse voice:

"'There-you'll-find-your-brother! There-you'll find-your-brother!'

"Sure enough, Brer Fox looked over the bank, and there was another Fox looking at him out of the water. Then he reached out to shake hands with him and in he went, heels over head, and Brer Tarrypin bubbled out:

"'I-doom-er-ker-kum-mer-ker!'"

"Was the fox drowned, Uncle Remus?" asked the little boy.

"He wasn't drowned exactly, honey," replied the old man, with an air of cautious reserve. "He did manage to scramble out, but a little more and the Mud Turtle would have got him, and then he would have been made hash of, world without end."

XIII

One goes a-hunting, but another bags the Game

FTER BRER Fox heard how Brer Rabbit had served Brer Wolf,"
said Uncle Remus, scratching his head with the point of his
awl, "he declared that he had better not be so hasty, and he let
Brer Rabbit alone. They were always seeing each other, and many
times Brer Fox could have caught Brer Rabbit, but every time that he
had the chance he remembered Brer Wolf, and he let Brer Rabbit
alone. By and by they got quite on good terms with each other as they
had been before, and it got so that Brer Fox would call on Brer Rabbit,
and they would sit and smoke their pipes, just as if no harsh feelings
had ever been between them.

"At last, one day, Brer Fox came and asked Brer Rabbit to go out
hunting with him, but Brer Rabbit felt rather lazy, and he told Brer Fox
that he had other fish to fry. Brer Fox felt very sorry, but he said that he
would try his hand anyhow, so off he went. He was gone all day, and
he had a wonderful stroke of luck, and bagged any amount of game.
By and by, toward the end of the evening, Brer Rabbit stretched himself, and said that it was about time for Brer Fox to be coming home.
Then Brer Rabbit mounted a stump to see if he could hear anything of
him. He wasn't there long before, sure enough, Brer Fox came through
the woods, singing like a drunk at a merrymaking. Brer Rabbit got
down from the stump and lay in the road, just as if he were dead. Brer
Fox came along and saw Brer Rabbit lying there. He turned him over
and examined him, and said:

"'This rabbit is dead. He looks as if he has been dead a long time.
He is dead, but he is very fat. He is the fattest rabbit that I have ever

seen, but he has been dead too long. I am afraid to take him home.'

"Brer Rabbit didn't say anything. Brer Fox licked his lips, but he went on and left Brer Rabbit lying in the road. Directly he was out of sight, Brer Rabbit jumped up, and ran around through the woods and got before Brer Fox again. Brer Fox came up, and there lay Brer Rabbit, apparently cold and stiff. Brer Fox looked at Brer Rabbit, and he thought for a minute or two. After a while he unslung his game-bag, and said to himself:

"'These rabbits are going to waste. I'll just leave my game here, and I'll go back and get that other rabbit, and I'll make folks believe that I'm old man Hunter from Huntsville.'

"And with that he dropped his game and trotted back up the road after the other rabbit. When he got out of sight, old Brer Rabbit snatched up Brer Fox's game and put out for home. The next time he saw Brer Fox he shouted:

"'What did you kill the other day, Brer Fox?'

"Then Brer Fox combed his side with his tongue, and answered:

"' I caught a handful of hard sense, Brer Rabbit.'

"Then old Brer Rabbit laughed, and said:

"'If I had known that you were after that, Brer Fox, I would have lent you some of mine.'"

XIV

BRER RABBIT IS A GOOD FISHERMAN

RER FOX and Brer Rabbit were like some children that I know of," said Uncle Remus, regarding the little boy, who had come to hear another story, with an affectation of great solemnity. "Each one of them was always after the other, playing tricks and interfering. However, Brer Rabbit did get some peace, because Brer Fox had become too scared to try any more pranks on Brer Rabbit.

"One day, when Brer Rabbit, Brer Fox, Brer Coon, Brer Bear, and a whole lot of them were clearing some new ground so as to plant a patch of Indian corn, the sun began to get rather hot, and Brer Rabbit felt tired. He didn't tell the others, however, because he was afraid that they would say he was lazy, so he kept on carrying off the rubbish, and piling up the brushwood until presently he exclaimed that he had got a thorn in his hand. He took this chance to slip off and find a cool resting-place. After a while he came to a well with a bucket hanging in it.

"'That looks cool,' said Brer Rabbit, 'and cool I expect it is. I'll just get in there and take a nap.' With that, in he jumped, and he had no sooner settled himself than the bucket began to go down."

"Wasn't the rabbit scared, Uncle Remus?" asked the little boy.

"Honey, there hasn't been a creature more scared since the world began than this Brer Rabbit. He fairly shivered. He knew where he came from, but he didn't know where he was going. Soon he felt the bucket touch the water, and there it stayed, but Brer Rabbit kept very still, because he didn't know what minute was going to be the next. He just lay there and shook and shivered.

"Brer Fox always had one eye on Brer Rabbit, and when he slipped off from the new ground, Brer Fox sneaked after him. He knew that Brer Rabbit was up to some game or other, and he crept off and watched him. Brer Fox saw Brer Rabbit come to the well and stop, and then he saw him jump in the bucket. After that, when Brer Fox saw him go down out of sight, he was the most astonished fox that you ever beheld. He sat there in the bushes and thought over it, but he couldn't make head or tail of the business. Then he said to himself:

"'Well, if this doesn't beat all that I ever saw or heard, then Joe's dead and Sal's a widow. Down in that well Brer Rabbit keeps his money hidden, and if it isn't that, then he must have discovered a goldmine, and if it isn't that, then I'm going to see what it is.'

"Brer Fox crept up a little nearer and listened, but he didn't hear anything. He kept getting nearer, but yet he didn't hear anything. Presently he got up close and peeped down, but he couldn't see or hear anything. All this time Brer Rabbit was very nearly scared out of his skin, and he was afraid to move because the bucket might tip over and then he would fall into the water. While he was saying his prayers as fast as a railway train running along the line, old Brer Fox shouted:

"'Hullo, Brer Rabbit? Who are you visiting down there?'

"'Who? Me? Ah, I'm just fishing, Brer Fox,' said Brer Rabbit. 'I said to myself that I would give you all a surprise with fish for dinner, so here I am and here are the fishes. I'm fishing for carp, Brer Fox.'

"'Are there many of them down there, Brer Rabbit?' asked Brer Fox.

"'Lots of them, Brer Fox; scores and scores of them. The water is alive with them. Come down and help me haul them in, Brer Fox,' said Brer Rabbit.

"'How am I going to get down, Brer Rabbit?'

"'Jump into the bucket, Brer Fox. It will bring you down safe and sound.'

"'Good-bye, Brer Fox, take care of your clothes,
For this is the way the round world goes;
Some go up and some go down,
You'll get to the bottom all safe and sound.'

"When Brer Rabbit got out, he galloped off and told the folks to whom the well belonged that Brer Fox was down there making all the drinking water muddy. Then he galloped back to the well, and shouted down to Brer Fox:

"'Here comes a man with a great big gun
When he hauls you up, you jump and run.'"

"What then, Uncle Remus?" asked the little boy, as the old man paused.

"In just about half an hour, honey, both of them were back in the new ground working as if they had never heard of any well, except that every now and then Brer Rabbit would burst out laughing, and old Brer Fox would get a fit of the dry grins."

XV

BRER RABBIT NIBBLES UP THE BUTTER

THE ANIMALS and beasts," said Uncle Remus, shaking his coffee around in the bottom of his tin cup, in order to gather up all the sugar, "they kept getting more and more friendly with one another, until Brer Rabbit, Brer Fox, and Brer Possum got to living together in the same shanty. After a while the roof sprang a leak, and one day Brer Rabbit, Brer Fox, and Brer Possum got together to see if they couldn't contrive to patch it up. They had a big day's work in front of them, and they brought their dinner with them. They put all the food in one pile, and the butter which Brer Fox brought was put in the springhouse to keep it cool. Then they set to work, and it wasn't long before Brer Rabbit's stomach began to trouble him. That butter of Brer Fox was heavy on his mind, and his mouth would water every time he thought about it. Presently he said to himself that he must have a nip at that butter, and so he made his plans. So while they were all working together, Brer Rabbit raised his head all of a sudden, flung his ears forward, and shouted:

"'Here I am. What do you want with me?' and off he went as if something was after him.

"He ran around, and when he had made sure that nobody was following him, he bounced into the spring-house, and there he stayed until he had had some butter. Then he sauntered back and set to work again.

"'Where have you been?' said Brer Fox.

"'I heard my children calling me,' said Brer Rabbit, 'and I had to

48

One goes a-hunting, but another bags the game

see what it was they wanted. My wife has been taken very ill.'

"They went on working, but that butter tasted so good that old Brer Rabbit wanted some more. So he raised his head, and shouted:

"'Hullo! Hold on! I'm coming!' and off he went.

"This time he stayed a good long time, and when he got back Brer Fox asked him where he had been.

"'I have been to see my wife, and she is sinking,' said he.

"Presently Brer Rabbit heard them calling him again, and off he went. This time he got that butter out so clean that he could see himself in the bottom of the bucket. He scraped it clean and licked it dry, and then he went back to work as quietly as a thief whom the policemen had been after.

"'How is your wife this time?' said Brer Fox.

"'I am most obliged to you, Brer Fox,' said Brer Rabbit, 'but I am afraid that she is gone by now.'

"That made Brer Fox and Brer Possum feel sorry for poor Brer Rabbit.

"By and by, when dinner-time came, they all got out their food, but Brer Rabbit kept on looking lonely and miserable, so Brer Fox and Brer Possum looked around to see if they couldn't make Brer Rabbit feel splimmy."

"What is that, Uncle Remus?" asked the little boy.

"Splimmy-splammy, honey—just as if he was in a crowd—as if his wife wasn't so dead as she might have been. You know how folks get when they are where people are crying."

The little boy didn't know, fortunately for him, and Uncle Remus went on:

"Brer Fox and Brer Possum bustled and got out the provisions, and presently Brer Fox said:

"'Brer Possum, you run down to the spring and fetch the butter, and I'll stay here and lay the table.'

"Brer Possum ran off after the butter, and directly he came back with his ears quivering and his tongue hanging out. Brer Fox shouted:

"'What's the matter now, Brer Possum?'

"'You had all better come and see,' said Brer Possum. 'The last bit of that butter is gone completely.'

"'Where has it gone?' asked Brer Fox.

"'It looks as if it has dried up,' said Brer Possum.

"Then Brer Rabbit, looking rather solemn, said:

"'I expect that butter has melted in somebody's mouth.'

"Then they all went down to the spring with Brer Possum, and sure enough the butter was all gone. While they were talking about the affair, Brer Rabbit said that he saw tracks all around, and that if they all went to sleep he could catch the fellow who had stolen the butter. Then they all lay down, and Brer Fox and Brer Possum soon dropped off to sleep. Brer Rabbit, however, stayed awake, and when the time came he got up quietly and smeared Brer Possum's mouth with the butter on his paws. Then he ran off and nibbled the best part of the dinner which they had left. Afterward he came back and woke Brer Fox, showing him the butter on Brer Possum's mouth. They woke up Brer Possum and told him about it, but of course Brer Possum denied it to the end. Brer Fox was something of a lawyer and he argued it out in this way— Brer Possum was the first one at the butter, and the first one to miss it, and more than that there were the signs on his mouth. Brer Possum could see that they had got him in a corner, so he said that the best way to catch the man who stole the butter was to build a big heap of brushwood and set it afire. Then all were to try to jump over, and the one who fell in would be the one who stole the butter. Brer Fox and Brer Rabbit both agreed. They set to work and built the heap of brushwood. They built it high and they built it wide, and then they set it afire. When there was a good blaze, Brer Rabbit took the first turn. He stepped back, then looked around and giggled, and over he went as easily as a bird flying. Then came Brer Fox. He went back a little farther and spit on his hands. Then he made the jump, and came so near falling in that his tail caught afire. Haven't you ever seen a fox?" inquired Uncle Remus.

The little boy thought that probably he had, but he wouldn't commit himself.

"Well, then," continued the old man, "the next time that you see one of them, you take a good look and see whether the end of his tail isn't white. It's just as I tell you. They bear the scar of that brushwood pile down to this day. They are marked—that is what they are they are marked."

"And what about Brer Possum?" asked the little boy.

"Old Brer Possum took a running start, and came lumbering along, and he dropped—*kerblam!*— right in the middle of the fire. That was the last of old Brer Possum."

"But, Uncle Remus, Brer Possum didn't steal the butter after all," said the little boy, who was not at all satisfied with such summary injustice.

"That's what makes me say what I do, honey. In this world, many folks have to suffer for other folks' sins. It looks as if it is very wrong, but that is just the way things happen. Trouble seems as if she is waiting around the corner to catch one and all of us, honey."

XVI

BRER RABBIT FINDS HIS MATCH AT LAST

IT SEEMS to me that I said the other night that in those days when the creatures were sauntering just the same as folks, that none of them were smart enough to catch Brer Rabbit," remarked Uncle Remus.

"Yes," replied the little boy, "that is what you said."

"Well, then," continued the old man solemnly, "that is where my memory failed, because Brer Rabbit did get caught, and it cooled him down just like pouring spring water on a big fire."

"How was that, Uncle Remus?" asked the little boy.

"One day, when Brer Rabbit was going lippity-clipiting down the big road, he met old Brer Tarrypin. After they had passed the time of day, Brer Rabbit declared that he was much obliged to Brer Tarrypin for the hand he took in the rumpus that day down at Miss Meadows's."

"When he dropped off the water-shelf on the fox's head," suggested the little boy.

"That's the time, honey. Then Brer Tarrypin said that Brer Fox ran very fast that day, but that if he had been after him instead of Brer Rabbit, he would have caught him. Brer Rabbit said that he could have caught him himself, but he didn't care about leaving the ladies. They kept on talking, until presently they got to disputing about which was the swifter. Brer Rabbit said that he could outrun Brer Tarrypin, and Brer Tarrypin vowed that he could outrun Brer Rabbit. Up and down they had it, until Brer Tarrypin said that he had a fifty-dollar bill in the chink of the chimney at home, and that that bill had told him that he could beat Brer Rabbit in a fair race. Then Brer Rabbit said he had a fifty-dollar bill which said that he could leave Brer Tarrypin so far behind that he could sow barley as he went and it would be ripe enough to cut by the time Brer Tarrypin passed that way.

"Anyhow, they made the wager and they put up the money. Old Brer Buzzard was summoned to be the judge and the stakeholder, and it wasn't long before all arrangements were made. The race was a five-mile heat. The ground was measured off, and at the end of every mile a post was set up. Brer Rabbit was to run down the big road, while Brer Tarrypin said he preferred to gallop through the woods. People told him that he would get along faster in the road, but old Brer Tarrypin knew what he was doing. Miss Meadows and the girls and almost all the neighbours heard of the fun, and when the day came they determined to be on hand. Brer Rabbit went in training every day, and he skipped over the ground as merrily as a June cricket. Old Brer Tarrypin lay low in the swamp. He had a wife and four children and they were all exactly like the old man. Anybody who wanted to know one from the other had to take a spyglass, and even then it was easy to make a mistake.

"That was the way matters stood until the day of the race, and on that day old Brer Tarrypin, his wife, and his four children got up before sunrise and went to the place. Mrs Tarrypin took her place near the starting-post, and the children near the others, up to the last one of all, and there old Brer Tarrypin himself took his stand. By and by there came the people: Judge Buzzard came, and Miss Meadows and the girls came, and then there came Brer Rabbit with ribbons tied around his neck and streaming from his ears. The folks all went to the other end of the track to see how the race would end. When the time came Judge Buzzard strutted around, pulled out his watch, and shouted:

"'Gentlemen, are you ready?'

"Brer Rabbit said 'Yes,' and old Mrs Tarrypin cried 'Go!' from the edge of the woods. Brer Rabbit set out on the race, and old Mrs Tarrypin made for home. Judge Buzzard flew along to see that the race was run fairly. When Brer Rabbit got to the first mile-post one of the

Tarrypin children crawled out through the woods and made for the post. Brer Rabbit shouted:

"'Where are you, Brer Tarrypin?'

"'Here I come a-bulging,' said the Tarrypin.

"Brer Rabbit was so glad that he was ahead that he ran harder than ever, and the Tarrypin made for home. When he came to the next post, another Tarrypin crawled out of the woods.

"'Where are you, Brer Tarrypin?' said Brer Rabbit.

"'Here I come a-boiling,' said the Tarrypin.

"Brer Rabbit ran as hard as ever he could and came to the next post, and there was the Tarrypin. Then he came to the next, and there was the Tarrypin. He had one more mile to run, and he felt as if he was getting winded. Presently old Brer Tarrypin looked down the big road and saw Judge Buzzard flying along, so he knew that it was time for him to bestir himself. He scrambled out of the woods, and rolled across the ditch. Then he shuffled through the crowd of folks, got to the milepost, and crawled behind it. By and by here came Brer Rabbit. He looked around, and as he couldn't see Brer Tarrypin he squalled out:

"'Give me the money, Brer Buzzard! Give me the money.'

"Then Miss Meadows and the girls laughed fit to kill themselves, and old Brer Tarrypin raised himself from behind the post and said:

"'If you will give me time to catch my breath, ladies and gentlemen, one and all, I expect I'll finger that money myself,' said he, and sure enough Brer Tarrypin tied the purse around his neck and skedaddled off home."

"But, Uncle Remus," said the little boy dolefully, "that was cheating."

"Of course, honey. The creatures began to cheat, and then folks took it up, and it keeps on spreading. It is very catching, and you had better be careful, honey, that somebody doesn't cheat you before your hair is as grey as my own."

XVII

THE FATE OF LITTLE JACK SPARROW

YOU'LL TRAMPLE on that bark till it won't be fit to throw away, let alone to make horse-collars of," said Uncle Remus, as the little boy came running into his cabin out of the rain. All over the floor long strips of bark were spread, and these the old man was weaving into horse-collars.

"I'll sit down, Uncle Remus," said the little boy.

"Well, then, you had better, honey," responded the old man, "because I hate to have my bark trampled on."

For a few minutes the old man went on with his work, but with a solemn air altogether unusual. Once or twice he sighed deeply, and the sighs ended in a prolonged groan that seemed to the little boy to be the result of the most unspeakable mental agony. He knew from experience that he had done something which failed to meet the approval of Uncle Remus, and he tried to remember what it was, so as to frame an excuse, but his memory failed him. He could think of nothing he had done that was calculated to stir Uncle Remus's grief. He was not exactly seized with remorse, but he was very uneasy. Presently Uncle Remus looked at him in a sad and hopeless way, and asked:

"What is that rigmarole you have been telling Miss Sally about your little brother this morning?"

"Which, Uncle Remus?" asked the little boy, blushing guiltily.

"Just what I am asking you now. I heard Miss Sally say that she was going to give him a whipping, and then I knew that you had been telling tales about him."

"Well, Uncle Remus, he was pulling up your onions, and then he went and threw a stone at me," said the child plaintively.

"Let me tell you this," said the old man, laying down the section of horse-collar he had been plaiting, and looking hard at the little boy, "let me tell you this—tattlers and tale-bearers never come to any good. They never do. I have been mixing up with folks now for nearly eighty years, and I never saw a tattler come to a good end. And if old man Methuselah were living at this very day he would tell you the same, as sure as you are sitting there. You remember what happened to the little bird that went around tattling about Brer Rabbit?"

The little boy didn't remember, but he was very anxious to know, and he also wanted to know what kind of a bird it was that so disgraced itself.

"It was one of these uppish little Jack Sparrows, I expect," said the old man; "they were always interfering with other folks' business, and they keep at it to this very day, pecking here, and picking there, and scratching out yonder. One day, after he had been tricked by old Brer Tarrypin, Brer Rabbit was sitting down in the woods thinking how he could get even. He felt very lonely and very angry, Brer Rabbit did. It isn't put down in the tale, but I expect he used bad words and rampaged around a good deal. Anyhow, he was sitting there by himself, thinking and thinking till presently he jumped up and cried:

"'Well, at any rate, I can get the better of old Brer Fox, and I'm going to do it. I'll show Miss Meadows and the girls that I am the master of Brer Fox.'

"Jack Sparrow up in the tree heard Brer Rabbit, and he sang out:

"'I'm going to tell Brer Fox! I'm going to tell Brer Fox! Chick-a-biddy-wind-a-blowing-acorns-falling! I'm going to tell Brer Fox!'"

Uncle Remus accompanied the speech of the bird with a peculiar whistling sound in his throat, that was a marvellous imitation of a sparrow's chirp, and the little boy clapped his hands with delight, and insisted on a repetition.

"This rather frightened Brer Rabbit, and he hardly knew what he was going to do. Presently he hit on the idea that the first man to see

Brer Fox would have the first chance, so he ambled off toward home. He hadn't got far when who should he meet but Brer Fox himself. Then Brer Rabbit said:

"'What is this between you and me, Brer Fox? I hear that you are going to send me to destruction, take my family, and destroy my shanty.'

"Then Brer Fox got very mad.

"'Who has been telling you all this?' said he.

"Brer Rabbit pretended that he didn't want to tell, but Brer Fox insisted and insisted, till at last Brer Rabbit told Brer Fox that he heard Jack Sparrow say all this.

"'Of course,' said Brer Rabbit, 'when Brer Jack Sparrow told me that, I got in a rage, and I used such language that I am very glad there were no ladies near to hear me.'

"Brer Fox looked surprised, and then said that he expected that he had better be getting on. But bless your heart, honey, Brer Fox didn't get far before Jack Sparrow flipped down on a date-plum bush by the side of the road and chirped out:

"'Brer Fox! Oh, Brer Fox! Brer Fox!'

"Brer Fox cantered on and pretended that he didn't hear him. Then Jack Sparrow sang out again:

"'Brer Fox! Oh, Brer Fox! Hold on, Brer Fox! I have got some news for you. Wait, Brer Fox! It will astonish you.'

"Brer Fox pretended that he didn't see or hear Jack Sparrow, but by and by he lay down in the road, and stretched himself out as if he were arranging for a nap. The tattling Jack Sparrow flew along and kept calling Brer Fox, but Brer Fox said nothing. Then little Jack Sparrow hopped on the ground, and fluttered around among the rubbish. This seemed to attract Brer Fox's attention, and he looked at the tattling bird, who kept on calling:

"'I've got something to tell you, Brer Fox.'

"'Get on my tail, little Jack Sparrow,' said Brer Fox, 'because I'm deaf in one ear and I can't hear with the other. Get on my tail.'

"Then the little bird hopped on Brer Fox's tail.

"'Get on my back, little Jack Sparrow, because I'm deaf in one ear and I can't hear with the other.'

"Then the little bird hopped on his back.

"'Hop on my head, little Jack Sparrow, because I'm deaf in both ears.'

"Up hopped the little bird.

"'Hop on my tooth, little Jack Sparrow, because I'm deaf in one ear and I can't hear with the other.'

"The tattling little bird hopped on Brer Fox's tooth, and then—"

Here Uncle Remus paused, opened wide his mouth, and closed it again in a way that told the whole story.

"Did the Fox eat the bird all—all—up?" asked the little boy.

"Judge Bear came along the next day," replied Uncle Remus, "and he found some feathers, and from that word went round that old man Squinch Owl had caught another what's-his-name."

XVIII

How Brer Rabbit saved the Meat

NE TIME," said Uncle Remus, whetting his knife slowly and thoughtfully on the palm of his hand, and gazing reflectively in the fire—"one time Brer Wolf—"

"Why, Uncle Remus!" the little boy broke in, "I thought you said the rabbit scalded the wolf to death a long time ago."

The old man was fairly caught, and he knew it; but this made little difference to him. A frown gathered on his usually serene brow as he turned his gaze upon the child—a frown in which both scorn and indignation were visible. Then all at once he seemed to regain control of himself. The frown was chased away by a look of Christian resignation.

"There now! What did I tell you?" he exclaimed as if addressing a witness concealed under the bed. "Didn't I tell you so? Goodness me! If children aren't getting so that they know more than old folks. They will dispute with you and dispute with you, unless their mother calls them, and I expect it won't be long now before she will. Then I'll sit here in the chimney-corner and get some peace. When the old Miss was living," continued the old man, still addressing some imaginary person, "it was more than any of her children would dare to do to come here disputing with me, and Master John will tell you the same any day you ask him."

"Well, Uncle Remus, you know you said the rabbit poured hot water on the wolf and killed him," said the little boy.

The old man pretended not to hear. He was engaged in searching among some scraps of leather under his chair, and kept on talking to the imaginary person. Finally he found and drew forth a nicely plaited whip-thong with a red snapper all waxed and knotted.

"I was making a whip for a little chap," he continued with a sigh, "but, goodness me! before I can get it done, the little chap has grown up so that he knows more than I do."

The child's eyes filled with tears and his lips began to quiver, but he said nothing; whereupon Uncle Remus immediately melted.

"I declare," he said, reaching out and taking the little boy tenderly by the hand, "if you are not exactly like the old Miss when I brought the last news of the war. It's just like bringing up a ghost which you aren't afraid of."

Then there was a pause, the old man patting the little child's hand caressingly.

"You aren't angry, are you, honey?" Uncle Remus asked finally, "because if you are, I'm going out here to bang my head against the doorpost."

But the little boy wasn't angry. Uncle Remus had conquered him and he had conquered Uncle Remus in pretty much the same way before. But it was some time before Uncle Remus would go on with the story. He had to be coaxed. At last, however, he settled himself back in the chair and began:

"Of course, honey, it might have been old Brer Wolf, and it might have been another Brer Wolf; it might have been before he was caught, and it might have been afterward. As the tale was told to me I tell it to you. One time Brer Wolf was coming along home from a fishing expedition. He sauntered along the road with his string of fish across his shoulder, when all of a sudden old Miss Partridge hopped out of the bushes and fluttered right in front of Brer Wolf's nose. Brer Wolf said to himself that Miss Partridge was only trying to draw him away from her nest, and with that he laid down his fish and poked into the bushes from which old Miss Partridge had come. About that time Brer Rabbit happened to come along. There were the fishes, and there was Brer Rabbit, and in such a case what do you expect an independent man like Brer Rabbit to do? I can tell you this, that those fishes didn't stay where Brer Wolf put them, and that when Brer Wolf came back they were gone.

"Brer Wolf sat down and scratched his head. He thought and thought, and then it came over him that Brer Rabbit must have been along there. Then Brer Wolf made for Brer Rabbit's house, and when he got there he called him. Brer Rabbit didn't know anything at all about any fishes. Brer Wolf said that he believed that Brer Rabbit had those fishes. Brer Rabbit denied it up and down, but Brer Wolf stood to it that Brer Rabbit had those fishes. Brer Rabbit said that if Brer Wolf believed that he had those fishes then he gave Brer Wolf leave to kill the best cow that he had. Brer Wolf took Brer Rabbit at his word, and went off to the pasture and drove up the cattle and killed Brer Rabbit's best cow.

"Brer Rabbit hated to lose his cow, but he laid his plans. He told his children that he was going to have that beef yet. Brer Wolf had been taken up by the police before now and he was terribly afraid of them so very soon here came Brer Rabbit shouting and telling Brer Wolf that the police were after him.

"'You run and hide, Brer Wolf,' said Brer Rabbit, 'and I'll stay here and take care of the cow until you get back.'

"As soon as Brer Wolf heard talk of the police, he scrambled off into the bushes as if he had been shot out of a gun. And he was only just gone when Brer Rabbit whirled in and skinned the cow and salted the hide down. Then he cut up the carcass and stowed it away in the smoke-house, and he stuck the end of the cow's tail in the ground. After he had done all this he shouted for Brer Wolf:

"'Come here, Brer Wolf! Come here! Your cow is going in the ground! Come here!'

"When old Brer Wolf got there, which he did quickly enough, there was Brer Rabbit holding on to the end of the cow's tail to keep it from going into the ground. Brer Wolf caught hold, and they gave a pull or two, and then up came the tail. Then Brer Rabbit winked his off eye, and said:

"'There! the tail has pulled out and the cow is gone.'

"But Brer Wolf wasn't the man to give it up so easily. He got a spade, and a pick-axe, and a shovel, and he digged and digged for that cow till he could dig no more. Old Brer Rabbit sat there in his front porch and smoked his cigar. Every time old Brer Wolf stuck the pick-axe in the clay, Brer Rabbit giggled to his children:

"'He can dig and dig and dig, but there's no meat there! He can dig and dig and dig, but there's no meat there!'

"Because all this time the cow was lying piled up in his smoke-house, and he and his children were eating fried beef and onions whenever they had a fancy for it.

"Now then, honey, you take this whip," continued the old man, twining the leather thong around the little boy's neck, "and scamper up to the big house and tell Miss Sally to give you some of it the next time that she finds your tracks in the sugar-barrel."

XIX

BRER RABBIT MEETS HIS MATCH AGAIN

"THERE WAS another man that got the better of Brer Rabbit," said Uncle Remus as, by some mysterious process, he twisted a hog's bristle into the end of a piece of thread—an operation which the little boy watched with great interest. "In those days," continued the old man, "the creatures carried on matters just the same as the folks. They went into farming, and I expect, if the truth were told, that they kept shops and had meetings and tea-parties when the weather was suitable."

Uncle Remus evidently thought that the little boy wouldn't like to hear of any further discomfiture of Brer Rabbit, who had come to be a sort of a hero, and he was not mistaken.

"I thought the terrapin was the only one that had fooled the rabbit," said the little boy dismally.

"It's just as I tell you, honey. There is never a man so smart but what there is one still smarter. If old Brer Rabbit had never been caught, the neighbours would have taken him for a ghost, and in those days they burnt witches before you had time to squint. They did that."

"Who fooled the rabbit this time?" the little boy asked. When Uncle Remus had the bristle set in the thread, he proceeded with the story:

"At one time Brer Rabbit and old Brer Buzzard agreed to go into partnership and sow their crops together. It was a remarkably good year, and the produce turned out wonderfully well, but, by and by, when the time came to divide, it turned out that old Brer Buzzard got nothing. The crops were all gone, and there was nothing there to show for them. Brer Rabbit appeared to be in a worse fix than Brer Buzzard, and he moped and looked miserable, and said that he was afraid that he would be sold out.

"Brer Buzzard said nothing, but he thought a lot, and one day he came and shouted for Brer Rabbit, saying that he had found a fine rich goldmine across the river.

"'You come with me, Brer Rabbit,' said Brer Buzzard. 'I'll scratch and you can grab, and between the two of us we'll make short work of that gold-mine.'

"Brer Rabbit was most anxious to set to work, but he couldn't make out how he was to get across the water, because every time he got his feet wet all the family caught cold. Then he asked Brer Buzzard if he could tell him how to manage it, and Brer Buzzard said that he would carry Brer Rabbit across. With that Brer Buzzard squatted down and spread his wings. Brer Rabbit mounted and up they rose."

There was a pause.

"What did the Buzzard do then?" asked the little boy.

"They rose," continued Uncle Remus, "and when they alighted, they alighted on the top of the highest pine-tree. This pine-tree was growing on an island, and the island was in the middle of the river with deep water running all around. As soon as they alighted Brer Rabbit knew which way the wind was blowing, and by the time old Brer Buzzard got himself balanced on a bough, Brer Rabbit said:

"'While we are resting here, Brer Buzzard, and as you have been so good, I have something I should like to tell you. I have a gold-mine of my own, one which I made myself, and I expect we had better go back to mine before we bother about yours.'

"Then old Brer Buzzard laughed till he shook, and Brer Rabbit sang out:

"'Hold on, Brer Buzzard! Don't flap your wings when you laugh, because if you do, something will drop from here, and my gold-mine won't do you any good, and neither will yours do me any good.'

"But before they got down from there, Brer Rabbit confessed all about the crop, and he had to promise to divide everything fairly and squarely. So Brer Buzzard carried him back, and Brer Rabbit was weak in the knees for a month afterward."

XX

A STORY ABOUT THE LITTLE RABBITS

IND THEM where you will and when you may," remarked Uncle Remus with emphasis, "good children are always taken care of. There were Brer Rabbit's children, they obeyed their daddy and mammy from day's end to day's end. When old Brer Rabbit said 'Scoot,' they scooted, and when old Mrs Rabbit said 'Scat,' they scatted. They did that. And they kept their clothes clean, and didn't get smuts on their noses either."

Involuntarily the hand of the little boy went up to his face, and he scrubbed the end of his nose with his coat-sleeve.

"They were good children," continued the old man heartily, "and if they hadn't been good there was one time when there wouldn't have been any little Rabbits. That's what."

"What time was that, Uncle Remus?" the little boy asked.

"The time when Brer Fox dropped in at Brer Rabbit's house and found nobody home but the little Rabbits. Old Brer Rabbit was off somewhere robbing a cabbage-patch, and old Mrs Rabbit was at a party in the neighbourhood, and while the little Rabbits were playing hide-and-seek in dropped Brer Fox. The little Rabbits were so fat that they fairly made his mouth water, but he remembered Brer Wolf, and he was afraid to gobble them up unless he had some excuse. The little Rabbits were very frightened, and they huddled together and watched Brer Fox's motions. Brer Fox sat there and wondered what sort of an excuse he could make up. Presently he saw a great big stalk of sugar-cane standing in the corner, and, clearing his throat, he talked very loudly:

"'Here, you young Rabs, just come here and break me off a piece of that sweetening-tree,' and then he coughed.

"The little Rabbits got out the sugar-cane, and wrestled with it, and sweated over it, but it wasn't any use. They couldn't break it. Brer Fox pretended that he wasn't taking any notice, but he kept on shouting:

"'Hurry up there, Rabs! I'm waiting for you.'

"And the little Rabbits hustled around and wrestled with it, but they couldn't break it. Presently they heard a little bird singing on the top of the house, and the song that the little bird sang was this:

> "'Take your toofies, and gnaw it,
> Take your toofies and saw it,
> Saw it and gnaw it,
> And then you can break it.'

"Then the little Rabbits were very glad and they gnawed the cane almost before old Brer Fox could get his legs uncrossed. When they carried him the cane, Brer Fox sat and wondered how he could find another excuse for seizing one of them. By and by he got up and took down the sieve which was hanging on the wall, and he said:

"'Come here, Rabs! Take this sifter, and run down to the spring and fetch me some fresh water.'

"The little Rabbits ran down to the spring, and tried to dip up the water with the sifter, but of course it all ran out. It kept on running out, and presently the little Rabbits sat down and began to cry. Then the little bird sitting up in the tree began to sing, and this is the song which he sang:

> "'Sifter holds water the same as a tray,
> If you fill it with moss and daub it with clay.
> The fox gets more angry the longer you stay—
> So fill it with moss and daub it with clay.'

"Up they jumped, the little Rabbits did, and they fixed the sifter so that it wouldn't leak. Then they carried the water to old Brer Fox. Then Brer Fox got very angry and pointed out a big log of wood, telling the little Rabbits to put that on the fire. The little chaps got round the wood, and they worked so hard at it that they could see their own sins, but the wood didn't budge. Then they heard the little bird singing, and this is the song which he sang:

> "'Spit on your hands and tug it and haul it,
> And get behind it and push it and pole it,
> Spit on your hands and bend back and roll it.'

"And just about the time that they got the wood on the fire their daddy came skipping in, and the little bird flew away. Brer Fox saw that his game was up, and it wasn't long before he made an excuse and started to go.

"'You had better stay and take a snack with me, Brer Fox,' said Brer Rabbit. 'Since Brer Wolf left off coming and sitting up with me, I get so that I feel very lonesome these long nights.'

"But Brer Fox buttoned up his coat-collar tight and made for home. And that is what you had better do, honey, because I can see Miss Sally's shadow sailing backward and forward before the window and before you know where you are she will be expecting you."

XXI

BRER RABBIT AND BRER BEAR

THERE WAS one season," said Uncle Remus, pulling thoughtfully at his whiskers, "when Brer Fox said to himself that he expected he had better see about planting a peanut patch. No sooner were the words out of his mouth before the ground was broken up and the peanuts planted. Old Brer Rabbit sat by and watched what was going on. Then he shut one eye and sang to his children:

> "' Ti-yi! Tungalee!
> I eat a pea, I pick a pea.
> It grows in the ground, it grows so free;
> Ti-yi! the goober pea."

"Sure enough, when those peanuts began to get ripe, Brer Fox found that somebody had been among the vines. He got very angry, and had a suspicion of whom the somebody was. But Brer Rabbit covered his tracks so well that Brer Fox didn't know how to catch him. One day Brer Fox took a walk all around the ground-pea patch, and before long he found a crack in the fence where the rails had been worn quite smooth, so in that place he set a trap. He bent down a hickory sapling that was growing in the corner, then he tied one end of a piece of rope to the top, and in the other end he made a loop-knot and he fastened that with a catch right in the crack. The next morning when old Brer Rabbit came creeping through the crack the loop-knot caught him just behind the forelegs, the sapling flew up, and there he was betwixt heaven and earth. There he was left swinging, and he was afraid that he was going to fall. While he was hatching a tale that he could tell

68

Brer Fox, he heard something lumbering down the big road, and presently there came old Brer Bear ambling along from the place where he had found a hollow tree where the bees had nested. Brer Rabbit hailed him:

"'How do you do, Brer Bear?'

"Brer Bear looked around, and there he saw Brer Rabbit swinging from the sapling, so he said:

"'Hullo, Brer Rabbit! How are you this morning?'

"'Thanks, I'm middling, Brer Bear,' said Brer Rabbit.

"Then Brer Bear asked Brer Rabbit what he was doing up there in the elements, and Brer Rabbit answered that he was making a dollar a minute. Brer Bear asked him how. Brer Rabbit said that he was keeping the crows off from Brer Fox's ground-pea patch, and he asked Brer Bear if he would like to make a dollar a minute, because he had a wife and family to support and he would make such a fine scarecrow. Brer Bear said that he would take the job, and it wasn't long before Brer Bear was swinging there in the place of Brer Rabbit. Then Brer Rabbit hurried off to Brer Fox's house, and when he got there he sang out:

"'Brer Fox! Oh, Brer Fox! Come here, Brer Fox, and I'll show you the man who has been stealing your peanuts.'

"Brer Fox grabbed his walking-stick, and both of them went running back to the ground-pea patch. When they got there, sure enough, there was old Brer Bear.

"'Oh, yes! you are caught, are you?' said Brer Fox, and before Brer Bear could explain, Brer Rabbit jumped up and down and shouted:

"'Hit him in the mouth, Brer Fox; hit him in the mouth'; and Brer Fox drew back with the walking-stick and *blip!* he struck him, and every time that Brer Bear would try to explain, Brer Fox would shower down blows on him.

"While all this was going on, Brer Rabbit slipped away and got in a mud-hole, just leaving his eyes sticking out. He knew that Brer Bear would be coming after him. Sure enough, presently, there came Brer Bear down the road, and when he got to the mud-hole he said: 'How do you do, Brer Frog; have you seen Brer Rabbit go by?'

"'He has just gone by,' said Brer Rabbit, and old man Bear rushed down the road as fast as a frightened mule. Brer Rabbit then came out and dried himself in the sun, going home afterwards to his family the same as any other man."

"The bear didn't catch the rabbit, then?" inquired the little boy sleepily.

"Jump up from there, honey!" exclaimed Uncle Remus, by way of reply. "I haven't any time to sit here propping up your eyelids."

XXII

Brer Bear catches Old Brer Bullfrog

ELL, Uncle Remus," said the little boy, counting to see if he hadn't lost a marble somewhere, "the bear didn't catch the rabbit after, did he?"

"Now you are talking, honey," replied the old man, his earnest face breaking up into little eddies of smiles—"now you are talking indeed. You won't find Brer Bear ever catching Brer Rabbit. It is something like setting a mule to catch a humming-bird. But Brer Bear got himself into some more trouble, which appeared to be a very easy thing for him to do. If folks could make their living by getting into trouble," continued the old man, looking curiously at the little boy, "old Mrs Favers wouldn't be bothering your ma to lend her a cupful of her sugar every now and then; and it seems to me that I know a man who wouldn't be squatting here making these fish-baskets."

"How did the bear get into more trouble, Uncle Remus? "asked the little boy.

"Easily, honey. Brer Bear had the idea that it was old Brer Bullfrog who had fooled him, and he said that he would pay him out if it took him a year. But it wasn't a year; it wasn't a month; more than that, it was scarcely a week. One day Brer Bear was going home after taking some honey from a bee-tree, when, lo and behold, whom should he see but old Brer Bullfrog on the edge of a mudpuddle fast asleep! Brer Bear dropped his axe, crept up, reached out his paw, and scooped up old Brer Bullfrog in just this way." Here the old man used his hand ladle-fashion, by way of illustration. "He scooped him up, and there he was. When Brer Bear had fairly got him in his clutches, he sat down and talked to him.

"'How do you do, Brer Bullfrog, how do you do? And how is your family? I hope that they are all well, Brer Bullfrog, because today you have some business with me that will last you a very long time.'

"Brer Bullfrog didn't know what to say. He didn't know what it was all about, so he said nothing. Old Brer Bear kept running on:

"'You are the man who made a fool of me about Brer Rabbit the other day. You had your fun, Brer Bullfrog, and now I'll have mine.'

"Then Brer Bullfrog began to get frightened, and he said:

"'What have I been doing, Brer Bear? How have I made a fool of you?'

"Then Brer Bear laughed, and pretended that he didn't know, but he kept on talking:

"'Oh, no, Brer Bullfrog! You are not the man who stuck his head up out of the water and told me that Brer Rabbit had gone by. Oh, no! you are not the man. I'll be bound you are not. About that time you were at home with your family, where you always are. I don't know where you were, but I know where you are, and now it's between you and me. After the sun goes down today you won't make a fool of any more folks going along this road.'

"Of course, Brer Bullfrog didn't know what Brer Bear was driving at, but he realized that something had to be done, and that very soon, because Brer Bear had begun to snap his jaws together and foam at the mouth. So Brer Bullfrog cried:

"'Oh, please, Brer Bear! let me off this time, and I won't ever do it again. Oh, please, Brer Bear! do let me off this time, and I'll show you the fattest bee-tree in the woods.'

"Old Brer Bear champed his teeth and foamed at the mouth. Brer Bullfrog cried louder than ever:

"'Oh, please, Brer Bear! I won't ever do it again! Oh, please, Brer Bear! let me off this time!'

"But old Brer Bear said he was going to kill him, and he thought and thought how he could do for Brer Bullfrog. He knew that he couldn't drown him, and he hadn't got a fire to burn him, so he was very puzzled. Presently old Brer Bullfrog stopped crying and boo-hooing, and said:

"'If you are going to kill me, Brer Bear, carry me to that big flat rock out there on the edge of the mill-pond where I can see my family, and after I have seen them you can take your axe and squash me.'

"That looked so fair and square that Brer Bear agreed, so he took old Brer Bullfrog by one of his hind-legs, slung his axe over his shoulder, and set out for the big flat rock. When he got there he laid Brer Bullfrog down on the rock, and Brer Bullfrog pretended to be looking around for his folks. Then Brer Bear took a long breath, and picked up his axe. Then he spit on his hands, and drew back and came down on the rock—*pow!*"

"Did he kill the frog, Uncle Remus?" asked the little boy, as the old man paused to scoop up a thimbleful of glowing embers in his pipe.

"Indeed, that he didn't, honey. Between the time when Brer Bear raised his axe and the time when he came down with it, old Brer Bullfrog jumped up and dived down in the mill-pond, *kerblink-kerblunk!* And when he rose away out in the pond he was singing, and this is the song that he sang:

> "*'Ingle-go-jang, my joy, my joy—*
> *Ingle-go-jang, my joy!*
> *I'm right at home, my joy, my joy—*
> *Ingle-go-jang, my joy!'*"

"That's a very funny song," said the little boy.

"It may seem funny to you," said the old man, "but it wasn't funny in those days, and it wouldn't be funny now if folks knew as much about the Bullfrog language as they used to know. That's certain."

XXIII

How Brer Rabbit Lost his Bushy Tail

AT ONE TIME," said Uncle Remus, sighing heavily and settling himself back in his seat with an air of melancholy resignation—"at one time Brer Rabbit was going down the road shaking his big bushy tail, and feeling as pleased as a kingbird with a fresh insect." Here the old man paused and glanced at the little boy, but it was evident that the youngster had become so accustomed to the marvellous developments of Uncle Remus's stories that the extraordinary statement made no unusual impression on him. Therefore the old man began again, and this time in a louder and more insinuating tone:

"At one time old man Rabbit was going down the road shaking his long bushy tail, and feeling very important."

This was effective.

"Great goodness, Uncle Remus!" exclaimed the little boy in open-eyed wonder, "everybody knows that rabbits haven't got long bushy tails."

The old man shifted his position in his chair and allowed his head to drop forward until his whole appearance was suggestive of the deepest dejection; and this was intensified by a groan that seemed to be the result of great mental agony. Finally he spoke, but not as addressing himself to the little boy.

"I notice that those folks who make a great show of what they know are just the folks upon whom you, can place no dependence when the occasion comes. You hear one of them now. He has just accused me of saying that rabbits have got long bushy tails, when goodness knows that if I had dreamt that I would very soon have undreamt it."

"Well, but, Uncle Remus, you said rabbits had long bushy tails," said the little boy. "Now you know you did."

"If I am not making a mistake, I said that old Brer Rabbit was going down the road shaking his long bushy tail. That is what I said, and that I stand by."

The little boy looked puzzled, but he didn't say anything. After a while the old man continued:

"Now then, if that is agreed, I'm going on, and if it isn't agreed, then I'm going to pick up my cane and look after my own affairs. There's work that is crying out to be done."

The little boy remained quiet, and Uncle Remus proceeded:

"One day Brer Rabbit was going down the road shaking his long bushy tail, when whom should he meet but old Brer Fox ambling along with a string of fish! When they had passed the time of day with each other, Brer Rabbit opened the conversation by asking Brer Fox where he got that fine string of fish. Brer Fox replied that he had caught them. Brer Rabbit asked where, and Brer Fox said down at the creek. Brer Rabbit asked how, because in those days they were ever so fond of minnows. Then Brer Fox sat down on a log and told Brer Rabbit that all he had to do in order to get a big lot of minnows was to go to the creek after sunset, and drop his tail in the water, and sit there till daylight. Then he would be able to draw up a whole armful of fishes, and those that he didn't want he could fling back. That is where Brer Rabbit was had, because he set out that night and went fishing. The weather was rather cold, so Brer Rabbit got a bottle of brandy and set out for the creek. When he got there he picked out a good place, and sat down, letting his tail hang in the water. He sat and sat, and he drank his brandy. He thought that he was going to freeze, but day came by and by and there he was. He gave a pull and felt as if he were coming in two. He gave another jerk, and lo and behold, where was his tail?"

There was a long pause.

"Did it come off, Uncle Remus?" asked the little boy presently.

"It did that!" replied the old man with unction. "It did that, and that is what causes all these bobtail rabbits which you see hopping and ske-daddling through the woods."

"Are they all like that just because the old rabbit lost his tail in the creek?" asked the little boy.

"That's it, honey," replied the old man. "That is what they tell me. It looks as if they are obliged to take after their pa."

XXIV

BRER TARRYPIN SHOWS HIS STRENGTH

B RER TARRYPIN was the most artful man," said Uncle Remus, rubbing his hands together contemplatively, and chuckling to himself in a very significant manner; "he was the most artful man in the whole gang. He was that."

The little boy sat perfectly quiet, betraying no impatience when Uncle Remus paused to hunt, first in one pocket and then in another, for enough crumbs of tobacco to replenish his pipe. Presently the old man proceeded:

"One night Miss Meadows and the girls gave a party, and so many of the neighbours came in response to the invitation that they had to put the molasses in the wash-pot and build the fire in the yard. Brer Bear helped Miss Meadows bring in the wood, Brer Fox attended to the fire, Brer Wolf kept the dogs off, Brer Rabbit greased the bottom of the plates to keep the sugar-candy from sticking, and Brer Tarrypin climbed up in a chair, and said he would watch and see that the molasses didn't boil over. They were all there, and they weren't playing any pranks either, because Miss Meadows put her foot down, and said that when they came to her house they had to hang up a flag of truce at the front gate and abide by it.

"Well, then, while they were all sitting there and the molasses was a-boiling and a-blubbering, they started boasting of what they could do. Brer Rabbit said that he was the swiftest, but Brer Tarrypin rocked himself in the chair and watched the molasses. Brer Fox said that he was the sharpest, but Brer Tarrypin went on rocking himself in the chair. Brer Wolf said that he was the savagest, but Brer Tarrypin went on rocking. Brer Bear said that he was the strongest, but Brer Tarrypin kept on rocking. By and by he shut one eye, and said:

"'It seems as if the old hardshell is nowhere by the side of the others in this crowd, yet here I am. I'm the same man who showed Brer Rabbit that he isn't the swiftest; and I'm the same man that can show Brer Bear that he isn't the strongest.'

"Then they all laughed aloud, because Brer Bear looked stronger than an ox. Presently Miss Meadows asked Brer Tarrypin how he was going to do it.

"'Give me a good strong rope,' said Brer Tarrypin, 'and let me get in a puddle of water, and then let Brer Bear see if he can pull me out.'

"Then they all laughed again, and Brer Bear said: 'We haven't got a rope.'

"'No,' said Brer Tarrypin, 'and neither have you got the strength,' and then he went on rocking himself, and watching the molasses a-boiling and a-blubbering.

"After a while Miss Meadows said that she would lend the young men her bed-cord, and while the candy was cooling in the plates they could all go out to the stream and see Brer Tarrypin carry out his project. Brer Tarrypin," continued Uncle Remus, in a tone at once confidential and argumentative, "wasn't much bigger than the palm of my hand, and it looked very funny indeed to hear him bragging of how he could outpull Brer Bear. But they got the bed-cord after a while, and then they all set out for the stream. When Brer Tarrypin found the place he wanted, he took one end of the bed-cord, and gave the other end to Brer Bear.

"'Now then, ladies and gentlemen,' said Brer Tarrypin, 'you all go with Brer Bear up there in the woods, and I'll stay here. When you hear me shout, that is the time for Brer Bear to see if he can haul in the slack of the rope. You all take care of that end, and I'll take care of this end.'

"Then they all set out and left Brer Tarrypin at the stream. When they were all safely gone, he dived down in the water and tied the bed-cord hard and fast to a big root, and then he rose and gave a whoop.

"Brer Bear wrapped the bed-cord around his hand, and winked at the girls. With that he gave a big jerk, but Brer Tarrypin didn't budge. Then he put both hands to it and gave a big pull, but all the same Brer Tarrypin didn't budge. Then he turned around and put the rope across his shoulders to try to walk off with Brer Tarrypin, but Brer Tarrypin looked as if he didn't feel like walking. Then Brer Wolf took a hand and helped Brer Bear to pull, but it was just as if he hadn't. Then they all helped him, and, goodness me! while they were all pulling, Brer Tarrypin shouted and asked them why they didn't take up the slack. Then when Brer Tarrypin felt them stop pulling, he dived down and untied the rope, and by the time they got to the stream he was sitting at the edge of the water just the same as the next one, and he said:

"'That last pull you gave was a mighty stiff one. A little more and you would have had me. You are very strong, Brer Bear, and you pull like a yoke of oxen, but I had a better purchase.'

"Then Brer Bear's mouth began to water after the sweet-stuff and he said that he expected that the candy was ready, so off they went after it!"

"It's a wonder," said the little boy, after a while, "that the rope didn't break."

"Break?" exclaimed Uncle Remus, with a touch of indignation in his tone—"break? In those days Miss Meadows's bed-cord would have held a mule."

This put an end to whatever doubts the child might have entertained.

XXV

Why Brer Possum has no Hair on his Tail

I T SEEMS to me," said Uncle Remus, frowning, as the little boy came hopping and skipping into the old man's cabin, "that I saw a youngster about your size playing and making free with those Favers children yesterday, and when I saw that I dropped my axe, and I sat down just where you are sitting now, and I said to myself that it's about time for old Remus to clear out altogether. That's exactly what I said."

"Well, Uncle Remus, they called me," said the little boy in a penitent tone. "They came and called me, and said they had a pistol and some powder over there."

"There now!" exclaimed the old man indignantly. "There now! What have I been saying? It's a great blessing that you weren't brought home on a litter with both eyeballs hanging out and one ear clean gone; that's what it is! It's a great blessing. I was delighted the other day when I heard Miss Sally laying down the law about you and those Favers children, yet, lo and behold, the first news I know is that you are hand in glove with them. It's enough to make the old Miss rise out of her grave down there in Putmon County, and what your grandma wouldn't have stood, your ma and I aren't going to stand either. The next time that I hear of such a thing, right then and there I shall be bound to lay the case before Miss Sally. Those Faverses weren't of any account before the war, and they weren't of any account during the war, and they aren't of any account now. While my head is hot you are not going to mix yourself up with the riff-raff of creation."

The little boy made no further attempt to justify his conduct. He was a very wise little boy, and he knew that, in Uncle Remus's eyes, he had been guilty of a flagrant violation of the family code. Therefore, instead of attempting to justify himself, he pleaded guilty, and promised that he would never do so any more. After this there was a long silence, broken only by the vigorous style in which Uncle Remus puffed away at his pipe. This was the invariable result. Whenever the old man had occasion to reprimand the little boy—and the occasions were frequent—he would relapse into a dignified but stubborn silence. Presently the youngster drew forth from his pocket a long piece of candle. The sharp eyes of the old man saw it at once.

"Don't you tell me that Miss Sally gave you that," he exclaimed, "because she didn't. And I'll warrant that you had to be very sly before you got a chance to snatch up that piece of candle."

"Well, Uncle Remus," the little boy explained, "it was lying there all by itself, and I just thought I'd fetch it out to you."

"That's right, honey," said Uncle Remus, greatly mollified: "that's right, because one of those other servants would have had it by this time. They are very proud, some of those house-servants, but I notice that they don't let anything pass. They go about with their hands and their mouth open, and what one doesn't catch the other does."

There was another pause, and finally the little boy said:

"Uncle Remus, you know you promised today to tell me why the possum has no hair on his tail."

"Dear me, honey ! Haven't you forgotten that yet? It seems to me," continued the old man, leisurely refilling his pipe, "that it went something like this: One time old Brer Possum got so hungry that he was obliged to have a feed of date-plums. He was a very lazy man, old Brer Possum was, but presently his stomach began to growl and shout at him so that he had to rack around and hunt up something. While he was racking around, whom should he run up against but Brer Rabbit? They were very old friends. Brer Possum never bothered Brer Rabbit like the other beasts. They sat down by the side of the big road, and there they jabbered and talked one to the other, till by and by old Brer Possum told old Brer Rabbit that he was nearly famishing. Brer Rabbit, smacking his hands together, jumped up in the air and said he knew where Brer Possum could get any amount of date-plums. Brer Possum asked where, and Brer Rabbit said that it was over at Brer Bear's date-plum orchard."

"Did the bear have a date-plum orchard, Uncle Remus?" asked the little boy.

"Of course, honey, because in those days Brer Bear was a bee-hunter. He made his living finding bee-trees, and the way he found them was by planting some date-plum trees. The bees would come to suck the date-plums, and then old Brer Bear would watch where they went, so that he could come up with them. But never mind about that; the date-plum patch was there just as I tell you, and old Brer Possum's mouth began to water as soon as he heard tell of it, so much that almost before Brer Rabbit had finished telling him the news Brer Possum set out. It wasn't long before he was perched up in the highest tree in Brer Bear's date-plum patch. But Brer Rabbit made up his mind to see some fun, and while all this was going on he ran around to Brer Bear's house, and told him that somebody was destroying his date-plums, so Brer Bear hustled off to catch him.

"Every now and then Brer Possum thought that he heard Brer Bear coming, but he kept on saying to himself:

"'Just one more date-plum and then I'll go; one date-plum more and then I'll go.'

"At last he heard old Brer Bear coming sure enough, but it was the same old tune 'One date-plum more and then I'll go.' And just about that time Brer Bear rushed into the patch, and gave the tree a shake, so that Brer Possum dropped out with the other ripe date-plums. By the time that he touched the ground, however, he got his feet together, and he made for the fence like a race-horse. Across that patch he and Brer Bear had it, and Brer Bear gained on him at every jump, till by the time that Brer Possum reached the fence Brer Bear grabbed him by the tail.

Brer Possum went between the rails and gave such a powerful jerk that he pulled his tail from between Brer Bear's tusks, but, lo and behold, Brer Bear held so tight, and Brer Possum pulled so hard that all the hair came off in Brer Bear's mouth, so that if Brer Rabbit had not happened to come up with some water Brer Bear would have been choked.

"From that day to this," said Uncle Remus, knocking the ashes carefully out of his pipe, "Brer Possum hasn't had any hair on his tail, and neither have any of his children."

XXVI

THE END OF BRER BEAR

THE NEXT time that the little boy sought Uncle Remus out, he found the old man unusually cheerful and good-humoured. His rheumatism had ceased to trouble him, and he was even disposed to be boisterous. He was finishing an axe-handle, and upon these occasions it was his custom to allow the child to hold one end while he applied sand-paper to the other. These relations were pretty soon established, to the mutual satisfaction of the parties most interested, and the old man began:

"When I see swell-headed folks like that woman who came and told your ma about your throwing things at her children, so that your ma got Master John to thrash you, it makes me think of old Brer Bear. Old Brer Bear suffered from swelled head."

"Was the bear's head sure enough swelled, Uncle Remus?"

"Now you are talking, honey!" exclaimed the old man.

"Goodness! what made it swell?"

This was Uncle Remus's cue. Applying the sandpaper to the axe-helve with gentle vigour, he began:

"One time when Brer Rabbit was going home from a party which they had been having at Miss Meadows's, whom should he meet but old Brer Bear. Of course, after what had passed between them there were no good feelings between Brer Rabbit and old Brer Bear, but Brer Rabbit was always careful of his manners, so he said:

"'Hullo, Brer Bear! how are you? I haven't seen you for ages. How are all at your house? How are Miss Brown and Miss Brindle?'"

"Who were they, Uncle Remus?" the little boy interrupted.

"Miss Brown and Miss Brindle? Miss Brown was Brer Bear's wife, and Miss Brindle was his daughter. That was what they called them in those days. So then Brer Rabbit asked him how he was, and Brer Bear replied that he was very poorly, and then they ambled along in quite a free-and-easy way. But Brer Rabbit all the time kept one eye on Brer Bear, and Brer Bear wondered how best he could nab Brer Rabbit. At last Brer Rabbit said:

"'Brer Bear, I have some business that would just suit you, I expect.'

"'What is that, Brer Rabbit?' said Brer Bear.

"'While I was weeding my new ground the day before yesterday,' said Brer Rabbit, 'I came across one of these old-time bee-trees. It was hollow at the bottom, and stayed hollow to the very top, and the honey was just oozing out. If you can put off your engagements to go with me, you'll get a feast that will last you and your family till the middle of next month.'

"Brer Bear said that he was much obliged and he believed that he would go. With that they set out for Brer Rabbit's new ground, which wasn't very far away. At any rate they got there after a while. Old Brer Bear declared that he could smell the honey. Brer Rabbit said that he could see the honeycomb. Brer Bear was sure that he could hear the bees humming. They stood there bragging in this way till presently Brer Rabbit said:

"'You do the climbing, Brer Bear, and I'll do the rushing around. You climb up to the hole, and I'll take this pine-pole and push the honey where you can get it.'

"Old Brer Bear spit on his hands, climbed up the tree, and put his head in the hole. Brer Rabbit grabbed the pine-pole, and the way he stirred up those bees was sinful—'that's what it was. It was sinful. And the bees swarmed on Brer Bear's head until before he could take it out of the hole it was swelled bigger than that dinner-pot. So there he swung, and old Brer Rabbit danced around and sang:

"*'The tree stands high, but the honey's very sweet—*
Watch those bees with stingers on their feet.'

"But there old Brer Bear hung, and if his head hasn't shrunk, I expect he's hanging there yet—that is what I expect."

XXVII

BRER FOX GETS INTO SERIOUS BUSINESS

IT HAPPENED at one time," said Uncle Remus, grinding some crumbs of tobacco between the palms of his hands, preparatory to enjoying his usual smoke after supper—"it happened at one time that Brer Rabbit made so free with the man's cabbage-patch that he set a trap for old Brer Rabbit."

"What man was that, Uncle Remus?" asked the little boy.

"Just a man, honey. That's all. That's all that I know. Nobody ever heard what his name was, or if they did they never told me. If this man must have a name, then I'm done, because you'll have to go to some-body else for it. If you are obliged to know more than I do, you will have to look for some one else that has sprung up since I commenced to shed my hair."

"Well, I just thought, Uncle Remus," said the little boy, in a tone re-markable for self-depreciation, "that the man had a name."

"To be sure," replied the old man, with unction, puffing away at his pipe. "Of course. That is what made me say what I did. This man might have had a name, and then again he might not. He might have been named Slipshot Sam, and he might have been named old One-eye Riley, but if he was it hasn't been told to me. But this man is in the tale and what are we going to do with him? That is the point, because when I start hunting in my memory after this Mister What-you-may-call-'em's name, it isn't there. Now then, let's call him Mr Man and let it go at that."

The silence of the little boy gave consent.

"One time," said Uncle Remus, carefully taking up the thread of the story where it had been dropped, "it happened that Brer Rabbit had been making so free with Mr Man's green-stuff that he set a trap for Brer Rabbit, and Brer Rabbit was so greedy that he walked right in it before he knew where he was. Well, it wasn't long before there came Mr Man browsing around, and he no sooner saw old Brer Rabbit than he smacked his hands together and said:

"'You are a pretty fellow, you are! You have been gobbling up my green-stuff, and now you are trying to carry off my trap. You are a very pretty fellow—that is what you are! But now that I have you, I'll just settle with you for old and new.'

"And with that Mr Man went off to look for some switches down in the bushes. Old Brer Rabbit didn't say anything, but he felt terribly lonely, and he sat there looking as if every minute was going to be the next. And while Mr Man was preparing his birches, who should come parading along but Brer Fox? Brer Fox made a great fuss about the fix in which he found Brer Rabbit, but Brer Rabbit began to laugh as if he would kill himself with laughing, and he told Brer Fox that Miss Meadows's folks wanted him to go down to the house to attend a wedding. He declared that he couldn't, and they declared that he could, until by and by they tied him there while they went after the parson, so that Brer Rabbit would be there when they came back. More than that, Brer Rabbit told Brer Fox that his children were very low with the fever, and that he was obliged to go after some pills for them, so he asked Brer Fox to take his place and go down to Miss Meadows's, where he could have a pleasant time with the girls. Brer Fox was always ready for a spree, and it wasn't long before Brer Rabbit had old Brer Fox harnessed up there in his place. He pretended that he had to make haste and get the pills for his sick children, and Brer Rabbit was only just out of sight when there came Mr Man with a handful of sticks. When he saw Brer Fox tied up there he was astonished.

"'Hullo!' said Mr Man, 'you have changed colour, and you have got bigger, and your tail has grown out. What kind of a what's-his-name are you, anyhow?'

"Brer Fox stayed still, and Mr Man went on talking:

"'It's great luck if, when I catch the chap who nibbles my greens, I likewise catch the chap who gnaws my goose,' he says, and with that he let out at Brer Fox with the sticks, and the way he dusted his jacket was a lesson to the whole neighbourhood. Brer Fox jerked and jumped and squealed and squalled, but Mr Man showered down on him as if he was fighting a wasps' nest."

The little boy laughed, and Uncle Remus supplemented this endorsement of his descriptive powers with a most infectious chuckle.

"By and by," continued the old man, "the switches got frayed out, and Mr Man went to get some more. When he had fairly gone out of hearing, Brer Rabbit showed up, because he had just been hiding in the bushes listening to the racket. He declared that it was very strange indeed that Miss Meadows hadn't come along, because he had been down to the doctor's house and that's farther than the parson's. Brer Rabbit then made as if he was hurrying off home, but Brer Fox said:

"'I'll thank you to set me loose, Brer Rabbit. I shall be much obliged if you will, because you have tied me up so tight that my head is swimming, and I don't expect I shall last to go down to Miss Meadows's.'

"Brer Rabbit sat down carelessly, and began to scratch one ear like a man thinking out something.

"'Is that so, Brer Fox?' said he. 'You do look rather done up. It looks as if something has been uncombing your hair.'

"Brer Fox said nothing, but Brer Rabbit kept on talking:

"'There aren't any bad feelings between us, are there, Brer Fox? Because if there are, I haven't time to waste here.'

"Brer Fox said that he didn't wish to have any unfriendliness, and with that Brer Rabbit cut Brer Fox loose just in time to hear Mr Man whistling up his dogs, and one went one way and the other went another."

XXVIII

Brer Fox and Miss Goose

IT HAD been raining all day, so that Uncle Remus found it impossible to go out. The storm had begun, the old man declared, just as the chickens were crowing for day, and it had continued almost without intermission. The dark grey clouds had blotted out the sun, and the leafless limbs of the tall oaks surrendered themselves drearily to the fantastic gusts that drove the drizzle fitfully before them. The lady to whom Uncle Remus belonged had been thoughtful of the old man, and 'Tildy, the house-girl, had been commissioned to carry him his meals. This arrangement came to the knowledge of the little boy at supper-time, and he lost no time in obtaining permission to accompany 'Tildy.

Uncle Remus made a great demonstration over the thoughtful kindness of Miss Sally.

"If she isn't one blessed white woman," he said, in his simple, fervent way, "then there isn't one of them around in these parts."

With that he addressed himself to the supper, while the little boy sat by and eyed him with that familiar curiosity common to children. Finally the youngster disturbed the old man with an inquiry:

"Uncle Remus, do geese stand on one leg all night, or do they sit down to sleep?"

"To be sure they do, honey; they sit down just as you do. Of course, they don't cross their legs," he added cautiously, "because they sit down flatfooted."

"Well, I saw one the other day, and he was standing on one foot, and I watched him and watched him, and he kept standing there."

"As to that," responded Uncle Remus, "they might stand on one foot and drop off to sleep and forget themselves. These geese," he continued, wiping the crumbs from his beard with his coat-tail, "are mighty curious fowls; they are mighty curious. In olden times they were among the bigbugs, and in those days when old Miss Goose gave a dinner all the quality was there. And they weren't stuck up either, because with all their fine style, Miss Goose wasn't too proud to take in washing for the neighbourhood, so she made money and got sleek and fat.

"That is the way matters stood when one day Brer Fox and Brer Rabbit were sitting up at the cotton-patch, one on one side of the fence, and the other on the other side, going on with one another, when all of a sudden they heard something—*blim, blim, blim!*

"Brer Fox asked what that noise was, and Brer Rabbit replied that it was old Miss Goose down at the spring. Then Brer Fox asked what she was doing, and Brer Rabbit said that she was battling clothes."

"Battling clothes, Uncle Remus?" said the little boy.

"That is what they called it in those days, honey. In these times they rub clothes on boards which have furrows in them, but in those days they just took the clothes and laid them out on a bench, and caught hold of the battling-stick and hammered the stuffing out of them.

"When Brer Fog heard that old Miss Goose was down there dabbling in soap-suds and washing clothes, he licked his lips, and declared that one of these long-come-shorts he would call and pay his respects. The minute he said that, Brer Rabbit knew that something was up, and he said to himself that he had better be by and have some fun while it was going on. Presently Brer Fox said to Brer Rabbit that he was obliged to be moving toward home, and with that they both said good-bye.

"Brer Fox set out to find his family, but Brer Rabbit slipped round and called on old Miss Goose. Old Miss Goose was down at the spring washing, and boiling, and battling clothes, but Brer Rabbit marched up and asked her how she was, and then she asked Brer Rabbit how he was.

"'I'd shake hands with you, Brer Rabbit,' said she, 'but they are all full of suds.'

"'That doesn't matter, Miss Goose,' said Brer Rabbit, 'as long as your will's good.'"

"A goose with hands, Uncle Remus!" the little boy exclaimed.

"How do you know that a goose hasn't hands?" Uncle Remus inquired, with a frown. "Have you been sleeping with old man Knowall? A little more and you will be telling me that snakes haven't feet, and yet if you take and lay a snake down here before the fire, the feet will come out before your eyes."

Uncle Remus paused here, but presently continued:

"After old Miss Goose and Brer Rabbit had passed the time of day with each other, Brer Rabbit asked her how she was in those days, and Miss Goose said that she was very poorly.

"'I'm getting stiff and I'm getting clumsy,' said she, 'and more than that, I'm getting blind. Just before you came along, Brer Rabbit, I dropped my spectacles in the tub, and if you had come along about that time, I declare I should have taken you for that nasty, audacious Brer Fox, and it would have been a born blessing if I hadn't scalded you with a pan of boiling suds. I'm so glad I found my spectacles that I don't know what to do,' said old Miss Goose.

"Then Brer Rabbit said that as Sis Goose had mentioned Brer Fox's name, he had something to tell her, and then he told her how Brer Fox was going to call on her.

"'He's coming,' said Brer Rabbit, 'he's coming, sure enough, and when he comes it will be just before day.'

"With that, old Miss Goose wiped her hands on her apron, and put her spectacles up on her forehead, and looked as if she had trouble on her mind.

"'Laws-a-mercy!' said she, 'supposing he comes, Brer Rabbit! what am I going to do? And there isn't a man about the house neither.'

"Then Brer Rabbit shut one eye, and said:

"'Sis Goose, the time is come when you must roost high. You look as if you have got the dropsy, but don't mind that, because if you don't roost high you are done for.'

"Then old Miss Goose asked Brer Rabbit what she should do, and he told her that she must go home and tie-up a bundle of the white folks' clothes, and put them on the bed. Then she must fly up on a rafter, and let Brer Fox grab the clothes and run off with them.

"Old Miss Goose said that she was much obliged, and she took her things and waddled off home. That night she did as Brer Rabbit said with the bundle of clothes, and then she sent down word to Mr Dog, and Mr Dog came down and said that he would sit up with her.

"Just before day, there came Brer Fox creeping up. The door opened when he gave it a slight push, and on the bed he saw something white which he took for Miss Goose, so he grabbed it and ran. Just about that time Mr Dog sailed out from under the house, and if Brer Fox hadn't dropped the clothes he would have been caught. From that, word went around that Brer Fox had been trying to steal Miss Goose's clothes, and he came perilously near losing his standing at Miss Meadows's. To this day," Uncle Remus continued, preparing to fill his pipe, "Brer Fox believes that Brer Rabbit was the occasion of Mr Dog being in the neighbourhood at that time of night, and Brer Rabbit hasn't denied it. The bad feeling between Brer Fox and Mr Dog started then and there, and it has gone on until now they don't get in smelling distance of each other unless there is a row."

XXIX

BRER FOX CATCHES MR HORSE

HERE WAS a pause after the story of old Miss Goose. The culmination was hardly sensational enough to win the hearty applause of the little boy, and this fact appeared to have a depressing influence upon Uncle Remus. As he leaned slightly forward, gazing into the depths of the great fireplace, his attitude was one of pensiveness.

"I expect I have worn out my welcome at the big house," he said, after a while. "I am almost certain I have," he continued, setting himself resignedly in his deep-bottomed chair, "because the last time I was there I had my eye on Miss Sally nearly the whole of the time, and when you see Miss Sally bustling around arranging things on the mantelshelf, bouncing the chairs around, and brushing up dust where there isn't any dust, and flying around singing louder than usual, then I know I've done something to annoy her."

"Why, Uncle Remus!" exclaimed the little boy, "Mamma was just glad because I was feeling so good."

"It might have been that," the old man remarked, in a tone that was far from implying conviction. "If it wasn't that, then she was getting tired of seeing me lounging around up there night after night; and if it wasn't that, then she was waiting for a chance to lecture your pa. Oh, I knew Miss Sally long before your pa knew her!" exclaimed Uncle Remus, in response to the astonishment depicted upon the child's face; "I've known her since she was so high, and during all that time I haven't seen a more outspoken white woman than Miss Sally.

"But that's all neither here nor there. You can now run down here just as you used to do, and we can sit here and tell tales to amuse our-selves just as we used to do before you got that splinter in your foot.

"I remember one time"—with an infectious laugh—"when old Brer Rabbit got Brer Fox in almost worse trouble than a man has ever got in yet. That was when he made a fool of him about the horse. Haven't I ever told you about that? But no matter if I have. Hoecake isn't well done until it has been turned over a couple of times.

"Well, after Brer Fox had rested from keeping out of the way of Mr Dog, and was able to catch his breath, he said to himself that he would pay out old Brer Rabbit if it took a month; and that too on top of all the experience he had had with him. Brer Rabbit managed to get wind of this, and, one day, while he was going along wondering how he could hold his own with Brer Fox, he saw a great big horse lying stretched out on his side in the field. He crept up to see if the horse were dead. He crept up, and he crept round, and presently he saw the horse switch his tail, and then Brer Rabbit knew that he was not dead. With that, Brer Rabbit ran back to the big road, and almost the first man he saw go by was Brer Fox, so Brer Rabbit ran after him, and shouted:

"'Brer Fox! O Brer Fox! Come back! I have some good news for you. Come back, Brer Fox,' said he.

"Brer Fox turned around, and when he saw who was calling him he came galloping back, because it seemed that this was as good a time as any to nab Brer Rabbit; but before he got near enough to seize him, Brer Rabbit said:

"'Come on, Brer Fox! I have found a place where you can lay in enough fresh meat to last you well till the middle of next year.'

"Brer Fox asked whereabouts, and Brer Rabbit said over there in the field. Brer Fox asked what it was, and Brer Rabbit said that it was a whole horse lying on the ground where they could catch him and tie him. With that Brer Fox said that he would come, and so they set off.

"When they got there, sure enough, there lay the horse stretched out in the sun, fast asleep, and then Brer Fox and Brer Rabbit had a dispute about how they were going to fasten the horse so that he couldn't get loose. One said one way and the other said another way, and there they went at it, until after a while Brer Rabbit said:

"'The only plan that I know, Brer Fox, is for you to get down there and let me tie you to the horse's tail, and then, when he tries to get up, you can hold him down. If I were a big man like you, you might tie me to that horse's tail, and if I didn't hold him down, then Joe's dead and Sal's a widow. I know well that you can hold him down,' said Brer Rabbit, 'but still, if you are afraid, we had better drop the idea, and work out some other plan.'

"Brer Fox was rather doubtful about this, but he had to look big before Brer Rabbit, so he agreed to the plan. Then Brer Rabbit tied Brer Fox to the horse's tail, and after he had got him tied there hard and fast, he stepped back, put his hands akimbo, and said:

"'If ever there was a horse caught, then we have caught this one. It does look as if we had put the bridle on the wrong end, but I'll warrant that Brer Fox has got enough strength to hold him.'

"With that, Brer Rabbit cut a long switch and trimmed it, and when he had finished it he stepped up and gave the horse a rap-*pow!* The horse was so surprised at such goings-on that he made one jump, and landed on his feet. When he did that, there was Brer Fox dangling in the air. Brer Rabbit darted out of the way, and shouted:

"'Hold him down, Brer Fox! Hold him down! I'll stand here and see fair play. Hold him down, Brer Fox! Hold him down!'

"Of course, when the horse felt Brer Fox hanging there on to his tail, he thought that something curious was the matter, and this made him jump and rear all the more. He shook Brer Fox just like a rag in the wind, and Brer Rabbit jumped and shouted:

"'Hold him down, Brer Fox! Hold him down! You've got him now, sure enough! Keep your grip and hold him down!'

"The horse jumped and humped, and ripped and reared, and snorted and cavorted, but still Brer Fox hung on, and still Brer Rabbit skipped around and shouted:

"'Hold him down, Brer Fox! You've got him so that he can't escape.

Hold him down, Brer Fox!'

"By and by, when Brer Fox got a chance, he shouted back:

"'How in the name of goodness am I going to hold the horse down unless I can get my claws in the ground?'

"Then Brer Rabbit stood back a little farther and shouted a little louder:

"'Hold him down, Brer Fox! Hold him down! You've got him now, sure enough! Hold him down!'

"Presently the horse began to kick with his hind-legs, and before long he gave Brer Fox a blow in the stomach that fairly made him shriek. Then he kicked him again, and this time he broke the cord and sent Brer Fox a-whirling. Brer Rabbit kept on jumping and shouting:

"'Hold him down, Brer Fox!'"

"Was the fox killed, Uncle Remus?" asked the little boy.

"He wasn't exactly killed, honey," replied the old man, "but he was next door to it. He was all broken up, and while he was getting well it seemed to cross his mind that Brer Rabbit had played another game on him."

Brer Rabbit and Brer Bear

How Brer Rabbit lost his bushy tail

XXX

Brer Rabbit and the Little Girl

WHAT DID Brother Rabbit do after that?" the little boy asked
presently.

"Now, then, you don't want to push old Brer Rabbit too
close," replied Uncle Remus significantly. "He is a very tender-footed
creature, and the more you push him the farther he'll leave you."

There was prolonged silence in the old man's cabin, until, seeing
that the little boy was growing restless enough to cast several curious
glances in the direction of the tool-chest in the corner, Uncle Remus
lifted one leg over the other, scratched his head reflectively, and began:

"At one time, honey, after Brer Rabbit had been tramping around
hunting for some salad for his dinner, he found himself in the neighbourhood of Mr Man's house, and he passed along until he came to the
garden-gate. Near the gate he saw Little Girl playing around in the
sand. When Brer Rabbit looked between the garden-railings and saw
the green-stuff, his mouth began to water. Then he walked up to Little
Girl, pulled his forelock, bowed, scraped his foot, and talked most politely:

"'How do you do, Little Girl?' said Brer Rabbit; 'how are you?'

"Then the Little Girl said, 'How do you do?' and she asked Brer
Rabbit how he was. Brer Rabbit declared that he was very poorly, and
then he asked her if she was the Little Girl whose pa lived in the big
white house, and the Little Girl said she was. Brer Rabbit said that he
was very glad, because he had been there to see her pa, and that he had
sent him to tell the Little Girl that she must open the garden-gate so

that Brer Rabbit could get some green-stuff. Then the Little Girl ran around and opened the gate. With that Brer Rabbit hopped in, got a fine feed of greens, and hopped out again. When he was going, he made a bow and told the Little Girl that he was obliged, and after that he set out for home.

"The next day Brer Rabbit hid himself until he saw the Little Girl come out to play. Then he put up the same tale, and walked off with another fine feed of greens. He kept on doing this, until presently Mr Man began to miss his greens. He kept on missing them, until he got to accusing everybody on the place of taking them, and when that came to pass the Little Girl said:

"'My goodness, pa! you told Mr Rabbit to come and make me let him in the garden after some greens, and hasn't he come and asked me, and haven't I let him in?'

"Mr Man had to think a long time before he saw how the land lay. Then he laughed, and told the Little Girl that he had quite forgotten about Mr Rabbit. Then he said to her:

"'The next time that Mr Rabbit comes, let him in, and then run as fast as you can and tell me, because I have some business with him that must be attended to.'

"Sure enough, next morning, there was the Little Girl playing around, and there came Brer Rabbit after his allowance of greens. He was ready with the same tale, and then the Little Girl let him in and ran up to the house, saying:

"'O pa! pa! O pa! Brer Rabbit is in the garden now! Here he is, pa!'

"Then Mr Man rushed out, grabbed up a fishing-line that was hanging in the back porch, and made for the garden. When he got there, there was Brer Rabbit trampling on the strawberry-bed and crushing the tomatoes. When Brer Rabbit saw Mr Man, he squatted down behind a cabbage leaf, but it wasn't any use. Mr Man had seen him, and before you could count eleven he had got hold Brer Rabbit tied hard and fast with the fishing-line. After he had got him tied safely, Mr Man stepped back and said:

"'You have fooled me many times, but this time you are mine. I'm going to take you and give you a thrashing, and then I'm going to skin you and nail your hide to the stable-door. To make sure that you get the right kind of thrashing, I'll just step up to the house and fetch the little red cowhide, and then I can warm your jacket.'

"Then Mr Man called to the Little Girl to watch Brer Rabbit while he was gone.

"Brer Rabbit said nothing, but Mr Man had only just gone out of the gate when he began to sing. In those days Brer Rabbit was a singer, I can tell you," continued Uncle Remus, with unusual emphasis, "and when he tuned up to sing he made the other creatures hold their breath."

"What did he sing, Uncle Remus?" asked the little boy.

"If I haven't forgotten that song," said Uncle Remus, looking over his spectacles at the fire, with a curious air of attempting to remember something, "it ran something like this:

> *"'The jay-bird hunted the sparrow's nest,*
> *The bee-martin sailed all 'round;*
> *The squirrel, he shouted from the top of the tree,*
> *Mr Mole, he stayed in the ground;*
> *He hid and he stayed till the dark dropped down—*
> *Mr Mole, he hid in the ground.'*

"When the Little Girl heard that, she laughed and asked Brer Rabbit to sing some more, but Brer Rabbit gave a cough, and declared that he was very hoarse somewhere down in his windpipe. The Little Girl persuaded and persuaded, and presently Brer Rabbit declared that he could dance even better than he could sing. Then the Little Girl asked him to dance, and Brer Rabbit said how in the name of goodness could a man dance while he was tied up in that way. The Little Girl said that she could untie him, and Brer Rabbit said that he didn't care if she did. With that the Little Girl reached down and untied the fishing-line, and Brer Rabbit stretched himself and looked around."

Here Uncle Remus paused and sighed, as though he had relieved his mind of a great burden. The little boy waited for a few minutes for the man to resume, and finally he asked:

"Did the rabbit dance, Uncle Remus?"

"Who? Him?" exclaimed the old man, with a queer affectation of elation. "Bless your heart, honey! Brer Rabbit gathered up his feet under him, he danced out of that garden, and he danced home. He did that! Surely you don't expect that an old hand who had had so much experience as Brer Rabbit was going to stay there and let Mr Man sacrifice him? *Shoo!* Brer Rabbit danced, but he danced home. Do you hear me?"

XXXI

How Brer Fox was too Smart

NCLE REMUS chuckled a moment over the escape of Brer Rabbit, and then turned his gaze upward toward the cobwebbed gloom that seemed to lie just beyond the rafters. He sat thus silent and serious a little while, but finally squared himself around in his chair and looked the little boy full in the face. The old man's countenance expressed a curious mixture of sorrow and resentment. Catching the child by the coat-sleeve, Uncle Remus pulled him gently to attract his attention.

"It seems to me," he said presently, in the tone of one approaching an unpleasant subject, "that no longer ago than yesterday I saw one of those Favers children climbing the big red oak out there, and then it seemed as if a little chap about your size tried to see if he couldn't be as smart as the Favers youngsters. I don't know why in the name of goodness you want to copy those Faverses. If you are going to copy other folks, copy those that are of some account. Your pa has the idea that all folks are equal, but Miss Sally knows better. She knows that there are no Faverses upon the top side of the earth that can compete with the Abercrombies in point of breeding and upbringing. That's what Miss Sally knows well enough. I've had my eye on those Faverses long before Miss Sally was born. Old Cajy Favers went to the poorhouse, and as to that Jim Favers, I'll be bound that he knows the inside of all the jails in this state of Georgia. They always hated black folks because they hadn't any, and they hate them down to this day.

"The year before last," Uncle Remus continued, "I heard your Uncle James Abercrombie tell that same Jim Favers that if he dared to touch one of his workers he would slap a load of buckshot into him; and, bless your heart, honey, your Uncle James was just the man to do it. But they are remarkably polite to me, the Faverses are," pursued the old man, allowing his indignation, which had risen to a white heat, to cool off, "and they had better be," he added spitefully, "because I know their pedigree from first to last, and when I get my African blood up, there's nobody, unless 'tis Miss Sally herself, who can keep me down.

"But that's neither here nor there," said Uncle Remus, renewing his attack upon the little boy. "What do you want to copy those Favers children for? You are sitting there this minute, thinking to yourself that I'm not going to tell Miss Sally, and that's just where you are making a big mistake. I'm going to let it pass this time, but the very next time I catch you anywhere near those Faverses, right then and there I shall go and tell Miss Sally, and if she doesn't give you a good whipping, then she is very different from what she used to be.

"All this trying to copy the Faverses puts me in mind of the time when Brer Fox tried to copy Brer Rabbit. I have already told you of the time when Brer Rabbit got the game from Brer Fox by pretending that he was dead, haven't I?"

The little boy remembered it very distinctly, and said as much.

"Well, then, when he saw how smartly Brer Rabbit made this trick work, old Brer Fox said to himself that he believed he would try the same game on some other man, and he kept on the look-out for a chance. One day he heard Mr Man coming down the big road on a one-horse wagon, carrying some chickens, some eggs, and some butter to town. Brer Fox heard him coming, and what did he do but to lie down in the road in front of the wagon. Mr Man drove along, clucking to the horse and humming to himself, and when they got almost up to Brer Fox the horse shied. Mr Man shouted 'Wo!' and the horse stopped. Then Mr Man looked down and saw Brer Fox lying there on the ground just as if he were cold and stiff. When Mr Man saw this, he exclaimed:

"'Hullo! There is the fellow who has been stealing my chickens, and somebody has shot him with a gun. I only wish it had been two guns—that I do!'

"With that Mr Man drove on and left Brer Fox lying there. Then Brer Fox got up and ran through the woods and lay down in front of Mr Man again. As Mr Man came driving along he saw Brer Fox, and he said: 'Hullo! Here is the very fellow that has been destroying my pigs. Somebody has killed him, and I only wish that they had killed him a long time ago.'

"Then Mr Man drove on, and the wheel of the wagon came very near smashing Brer Fox's nose; yet all the same Brer Fox leapt up and ran around ahead of Mr Man, and lay down in the road. When Mr Man came along there he was stretched out looking big enough to fill a two-bushel basket, and just right to be skinned. Mr Man drove up and then stopped. He looked down at Brer Fox, and then he had a good look around to see if he could find the reason for all these dead foxes. Mr Man looked all around, but he neither saw nor heard anything. Then he sat there and thought, and presently he said to himself that he had better see what kind of disease it was that had got into Brer Fox's family. With that he got down out of the wagon and felt Brer Fox's ear; it felt quite warm. Then he felt Brer Fox's neck; it felt quite warm. Then he felt Brer Fox in the short ribs; Brer Fox was sound in the short ribs. Then he felt Brer Fox's limbs; Brer Fox was sound in the limbs. Then he turned Brer Fox over, and, lo and behold, Brer Fox felt quite soft. When Mr Man saw this, he said to himself:

"'Hullo! what is the meaning of this? This chicken-stealer looks as if he is dead, but there aren't any bones broken, I haven't seen any blood, nor have I felt any bruise. More than that, he is warm and soft. There is certainly something wrong here. This pig-stealer *might* be dead, and then again he might not be dead, so to make sure that he is, I'll just give him a whack with the handle of my whip.' With that Mr Man drew back and gave Brer Fox a clip behind his ears—*pow!*—and the blow came so hard and so quickly that Brer Fox thought for certain he would never be able to get up again; but before Mr Man could draw back to give him another cut, Brer Fox scrambled to his feet, and made tracks away from there."

Uncle Remus paused, and shook the cold ashes from his pipe, and then applied the moral:

"That's what Brer Fox got for playing Mr Smarty and copying other folks, and that is what happens to all the Smarty family."

XXXII

BRER RABBIT'S ASTONISHING PRANK

I EXPECT THAT was why old Brer Rabbit got on so well. He didn't copy the other creatures," Uncle Remus continued after a while. "When he disappeared from them, he always went to a fresh place. They didn't know where to look for him. He was the funniest creature of the whole gang. Some folks might have called him lucky, and yet, even when he had bad luck, he usually came out on top. It seems very strange now, but it wasn't at all strange then, because everybody agreed that whenever and wherever you found him, Brer Rabbit was the artfulest of all the creatures.

"At one time old Brer Rabbit had an idea that he would like to pay Brer Bear a call. No sooner did the notion strike him than he picked himself up and made for Brer Bear's house."

"Why, I thought they were mad with each other," the little boy exclaimed.

"Brer Rabbit made his call when Brer Bear and his family were away from home," Uncle Remus explained, with a chuckle which was in the nature of a hearty tribute to the crafty judgment of Brer Rabbit.

"He sat down in the road, and he saw them go by—old Brer Bear and old Mrs Bear, and their two twin children, one of whom was called Kubs and the other Klibs."

The little boy laughed, but the severe seriousness of Uncle Remus would have served for a study as he continued:

"Old Brer Bear and old Mrs Bear went along ahead, and Kubs and Klibs came shuffling and scrambling on behind. When Brer Rabbit saw this, he said to himself that he had better go and see how Brer

Bear was getting on, and off he went. It wasn't long before he was ransacking the premises just as if he were a policeman. While he was going around peeping here and poking there, he began rummaging among the shelves, and a bucket of honey which Brer Bear had hidden in the cupboard fell down and spilled on top of Brer Rabbit. A little more and he would have been drowned. From head to heels that creature was covered in honey: he wasn't just smeared with it, he was totally covered. He had to sit there and let the sweetness drop out of his eyes before he could see his hand before him, and then after he had looked around a little he said to himself:

"'Hullo! What am I going to do now? If I go out in the sunshine the bumble-bees and the flies will swarm up and take me, and if I stay here Brer Bear will come back and catch me. I don't know what in the name of goodness I am going to do.'

"However, presently a notion struck Brer Rabbit, and he tiptoed along until he got in the woods. Then what did he do but roll himself in the leaves and rubbish to try to rub the honey off that way. He rolled, and the leaves stuck. Brer Rabbit rolled more, and the leaves stuck more. He kept on rolling and the leaves kept on sticking, until after a while Brer Rabbit was the most extraordinary creature that you have ever set eyes on. If Miss Meadows and the girls could have seen him that day they would never have let Brer Rabbit call at their house again. No, indeed they wouldn't.

"Brer Rabbit jumped around, and tried to shake the leaves off, but the leaves were not going to be shaken off. Brer Rabbit shook and shivered, but still the leaves stuck: and the capers that creature cut there in the woods all by himself were scandalous—that they were, they were scandalous.

"Brer Rabbit saw that this wouldn't do, so he said to himself that he had better make for home, so off he went. I expect you have heard of those bogy-men who come after naughty children," continued Uncle Remus, in a tone so seriously confidential as to be altogether depressing; "well, then, that was just how Brer Rabbit looked, and if you had seen him you would have been sure that he was the grandfather of all the bogy-men. Brer Rabbit paced along, and with every motion that he made the leaves went *swishy-swushy*, *splushy-splishy*, and, from the fuss which he made and the way he looked, you would have taken him for the savagest creature who had gone from the face of the earth since Noah let down the drawbars of the ark and turned the animals loose. I'll be bound that if you had met him you would have been very glad indeed to have got away before anything happened to you.

"The first person whom Brer Rabbit met was old Sis Cow, and no sooner did she set eyes on him than she hoisted her tail in the air and ran off as if a pack of dogs were after her. This made Brer Rabbit laugh. He knew that when an old and staid woman like Sis Cow runs like a mad creature in the broad daylight there must be something very curious about those leaves and that honey, so he went on racing down the road. The next person he met was a black girl leading a number of little pigs. When that girl saw Brer Rabbit come prancing along, she flung down her basket of corn and fairly flew, and the little pigs went through the woods, and the noise they made with their running and their snorting and the squealing has never been heard in that settlement before or since. Things went on in this way every time that Brer Rabbit met anybody—they just ran off as if the Old Boy was after them.

"Of course this made Brer Rabbit feel very important, and he declared that he had better skirmish in the neighbourhood of Brer Fox's house. While he was standing there going over all this in his mind, who should come along but Brer Bear and his family. Brer Rabbit got crossways in the road and sidled toward them. Old Brer Bear stopped and looked, but Brer Rabbit kept on sidling toward them. Old Mrs Bear stood it as long as she could, and then she flung down her parasol and went up a tree. Brer Bear seemed as if he was going to stand his ground, but Brer Rabbit jumped straight up in the air, giving himself a shake, and, bless your heart, honey! old Brer Bear made a dash, and they tell me he tore down a whole length of fence in his hurry to get away from there. As to Kubs and Klibs, they took their hats in their hands and skedaddled through the woods like a drove of horses."

"And then what?" the little boy asked.

"Brer Rabbit paraded down the road," continued Uncle Remus; "and presently there came Brer Fox and Brer Wolf, making a plan to catch Brer Rabbit, and they were so intent on their conversation that they got quite close to Brer Rabbit before they saw him, but when they did catch a glimpse of him, they gave him all the room he wanted, I can tell you. Brer Wolf tried to show off, because he wished to look big in front of Brer Fox, and so he stopped to ask Brer Rabbit who he was. Brer Rabbit jumped up and down in the middle of the road, and shouted:

"'I'm the Will-o'-the-Wisp. I'm the Will-o'-the-Wisp, and you are the man I'm after!'

"Then Brer Rabbit jumped up and down, making as if he were going after Brer Fox and Brer Wolf, and the way those creatures set off from there was a caution.

"A long time after that," continued Uncle Remus, folding his hands placidly in his lap with the air of one who has performed a pleasant duty, "a long time after that, when Brer Rabbit came up with Brer Fox and Brer Wolf, he got behind a stump, and shouted:

"'I'm the Will-o'-the-Wisp, and you are the men I'm after!'

"Brer Fox and Brer Wolf ran, but before they got out of sight and hearing Brer Rabbit showed up and laughed fit to kill himself. Afterwards, Miss Meadows heard about it, and the next time that Brer Fox called, the girls giggled, and asked him if he wasn't afraid that the Will-o'-the-Wisp might drop in."

XXXIII

BRER RABBIT SECURES A MANSION

HE RAIN continued to fall the next day, but the little boy made arrangements to go with 'Tildy when she carried Uncle Remus his supper. This happened to be a waiter full of things left over from dinner. There was so much that the old man was moved to remark:

"I declare that it looks as if Miss Sally had got my name in the pot this time, for certain. I just wish you would look at that loaf of bread, honey, and those greens, and see if they haven't got Remus written somewhere on them. Those bits of chicken look as if they are good, but I'm not so used to them as to that boiled ham. Those sweet potatoes we can share between us, but the jam will fit your palate better than it will mine. This hunk of beef we will talk about when the time comes, but those biscuits I know Miss Sally put in for some little chap whose name I'm not going to say."

It was easy to perceive that the sight of the supper had put Uncle Remus in rare good-humour. He moved about briskly. taking the plates from the waiter and distributing them with exaggerated carefulness around upon his little pine-table. Meanwhile he kept up a running fire of conversation.

"Folks who can sit down and have their food brought to them and placed right under their noses—those folks don't need any umbrella. The night before last, while I was sitting there in the doorway, I heard those Willis-whistlers, and then I knew that we were going to get rain."

"The Willis-whistlers, Uncle Remus!" exclaimed the little boy. "What are they?"

"You are too hard for me now, honey. What I know I don't mind telling, but when you ask me about what I don't know, then you are too hard for me, for certain. These Willis-whistlers were before my time, and I've been knocking around in these parts for nearly eighty years now. Some people want to say that they are frogs, but I wish that they would explain to me how frogs can shout so that the nearer you come to them the farther away you are; I would be very glad if some one would tell me that. Many and many's the time that I've gone after these Willis-whistlers, and it doesn't matter where I go, they are always somewhere else. You can put the shovel in the fire and make the squinch owl be quiet, and you can put your hand on the trees and make the locust beetles stop their noise, but these Willis-whistlers are always away off yonder."

Suddenly Uncle Remus paused over one of the dishes, and exclaimed:

"Goodness gracious! Whatever is this that Miss Sally has sent us?"

"That," said the little boy, after making an investigation, "is what mamma calls a floating island."

"Well, then," Uncle Remus remarked, in a relieved tone, "that's different. I was afraid that it might be some of that syllabub, a whole jugful of which isn't enough to make you dream that you have had a drink. If I'm going to be fed on foam," continued the old man, by way of explaining his position on the subject of syllabub, "let it be foam, and if I'm going to have a drink, let me drink it down while there's some strength in it. That's me up and down. As for your floating island, give me a hunk of ginger-cake and a mug of date-plum beer, and you won't find a smarter man than I am.

"Miss Sally is a very curious white woman," Uncle Remus went on. "She has sent all these things down here, and I expect they are monstrous nice, but only last Tuesday she had all the folks in the place, big and little, calling for Remus. It was Remus here and Remus there, and, lo and behold, when I came to find out, Miss Sally wanted Remus to cook one of these old-time ash-cakes. She was obliged to have it then and there, and when I had done it, Miss Sally got a glass of buttermilk, and sat right down on the floor as she used to do when she was a little girl." The old man paused, straightened up, looked at the child over his spectacles, and continued with emphasis: "And I'm blest if she didn't eat a hunk of that ash-cake nearly as big as your head, and then she made out that it wasn't cooked right.

"Now then, honey, all this is arranged. You sit there and I'll sit here, and between us we'll sample these things and see what it is that Miss Sally has sent us. While we are making away with it, I'll brush up my memory, and see if I can call to mind the tale of how old Brer Rabbit got a two-story house without spending much money."

Uncle Remus stopped talking a little while and pretended to be trying to remember something— an effort that was accompanied by a curious humming sound in his throat. Finally he brightened up and began:

"It happened at one time that a whole lot of the creatures took the idea of going shares in building a house. Old Brer Bear was among them, and Brer Fox, and Brer Wolf, and Brer Coon, and Brer Possum. I can't be sure, but I fancy that old Brer Mink was one of them. Anyhow, there was a whole parcel of them, and they set about it and built a house in less than no time. Brer Rabbit pretended that it made his head swim to climb up on the scaffold. He also said that it made him catch the palsy if he worked in the sun. But he got a square and stuck a pencil behind his ear, and then he went around measuring and marking, measuring and marking, and he was so busy that the other creatures thought he was doing a monstrous lot of work. Folks going along the big road said that Brer Rabbit was doing more hard work than the whole crowd of them. Yet all this time Brer Rabbit was doing nothing, and he might just as well have been lying away in the shade scratching the fleas out of himself. The other creatures built the house, and indeed it was a fine one. It would have been a fine one in these days, let alone what it was in those times. There was upstairs and downstairs, and chimneys all around, and there were rooms for all the creatures who took shares and helped to build it.

"Brer Rabbit picked out one of the upstair rooms. Then he got a gun, and one of these brass cannons, and he put them in the room when the other creatures weren't looking. After that he got a tub of nasty dirty water which he likewise put in there when they weren't looking. So, when the house was finished, and while they were sitting in the parlour after supper, Brer Rabbit yawned and stretched himself as if he was very tired. Making his excuses, he said that he believed he would go to his room. When he got there, and while all the other creatures were laughing and chatting as sociably as you please, Brer Rabbit put his head out of the door of his room and sang out:

"'When a big man like me wants to sit down, whereabouts is he going to sit?'

"Then the other creatures laughed, and answered:

"'If a big man like you can't sit in a chair, he'd better sit down on the floor.'

"'Look out down there, then,' said Brer Rabbit, 'because I'm going to sit down.'

"With that, *bang!* went Brer Rabbit's gun. Of course this astonished the creatures, and they looked around at one another as much as to say, 'What in the name of goodness is that?' They listened, but they didn't hear any more disturbance, and it wasn't long before they got to chattering again. Presently Brer Rabbit put his head out of his room door and sang out:

"'When a big man like me wants to sneeze, whereabouts is he going to sneeze?'

"Then the other creatures shouted back:

"'If a big man like you hasn't lost his wits, he can sneeze wherever he pleases.'

"'Look out down there, then,' said Brer Rabbit, 'because I'm going to sneeze this very minute.'

"With that Brer Rabbit let off his cannon—*bulderum-m-m!* The glass in the windows shook and rattled as if it was going to fall out, and old Brer Bear fell out of the rocking-chair—*kerblump!* When the

Brer Tarrypin shows his strength

creatures settled down again, Brer Possum and Brer Mink declared that as Brer Rabbit had such a monstrous cold, they believed that they would step out and get some fresh air, but the other creatures said that they would put up with it, and after a while, when they smoothed their ruffled hair, they began to talk among themselves. When they had got well going again, Brer Rabbit sang out:

"'When a big man like me takes a chew of tobacco, whereabouts is he going to spit?'

"Then the other creatures shouted back, as if they were tired of this:

"'Big man or little man, spit where you please.'

"Then Brer Rabbit squalled:

"'This is the way a big man spits!' and with that he tilted the tub of dirty water, and when the other creatures heard it coming sloshing down the stairs, gentlemen! they just fled. Some went out of the back door, and some went out of the front door, and some fell out of the windows. Some went one way and some went another way, but they all went."

"But what became of Brer Rabbit?" the little boy asked.

"Brer Rabbit shut up the house and fastened the windows, and then he went to bed. After he had pulled the coverlet around his ears, he slept like a man who didn't owe anybody anything. Nor did he owe anything, because if the other creatures allowed themselves to be frightened out of their own house, what business was that of Brer Rabbit's? That is what I should like to know."

XXXIV

Mr Lion hunts for Mr Man

Uncle Remus sighed heavily as he lifted the trivet on the head of his walking-cane and hung it carefully by the side of the griddle in the cavernous fireplace.

"Folks may come along with the what-you-may call-'ems," he said presently, turning to the little boy, who was supplementing his supper by biting off a chew of shoemaker's-wax, "and likewise they can bring round their what's-his-names. They can walk biggity, and they can talk biggity, and what is more, they can feel biggity, but all the same they get caught. They go along, and they go along, and then presently trouble comes and gets hold of them, and the bigger they are the worse trouble gets hold of them."

The little boy didn't understand this harangue at all, but he appreciated it because he recognized it as the prelude to a story.

"There was Mr Lion," Uncle Remus went on; "he set himself up as the master of all the other creatures, and he felt so biggity that he went roaring and ramping around the neighbourhood worse than that speckled bull that you saw down at your Uncle James Abercrombie's place last year. He went roaring around, and everywhere he went he heard talk of Mr Man. In the very middle of his bragging some one would tell him about what Mr Man had done. Mr Lion would say that he had done this, and then he would hear of how Mr Man had done that. It went on in this way until presently Mr Lion shook his mane, and said that he was going to search round and round, high and low, to see if he couldn't find Mr Man. He declared too that when he did find him he was going to turn in and give Mr Man such a thrashing as no creature had ever had yet. The other creatures told Mr Lion that he had better leave Mr Man alone, but Mr Lion said that he was going to hunt him down in spite of all they could say.

"Sure enough, after he had taken some rest, Mr Lion set out down the big road. The sun arose and shone hot, but Mr Lion kept on. The wind blew, and filled the air with dust; the rain came on and drizzled down; but Mr Lion kept on. Presently, while he was going on in this way, with his tongue hanging out, he met Mr Steer, grazing by the side of the road. Mr Lion asked him how he was, most politely, and Mr Steer likewise bowed and scraped and showed his manners. Then Mr Lion made as if he wanted to have a little talk with him, and he said:

"'Is there anybody around in these parts named Mr Man?'

"'To be sure there is,' said Mr Steer; 'anybody can tell you that. I know him very well.'

"'Well, then, he's the very chap I'm after,' said Mr Lion.

"'What may be your business with Mr Man?' said Mr Steer.

"'I've come a long way on purpose to give him a thrashing,' said Mr Lion. 'I'm going to show him who is master in this neighbourhood.' And with that Mr Lion shook his mane, switched his tail, and strutted up and down as if he was one of these town men.

"'Well, then, if that is what you came after,' said Mr Steer, 'you had just better turn around and point your nose toward home, because you are now putting yourself in the way of getting into certain trouble.'

"'I'm going to thrash that same Mr Man,' said Mr Lion; 'I've come for that, and that is what I'm going to do.'

"Mr Steer drew a long breath, and chewed the cud very slowly. Then after a while he said:

"'You see me standing here right in front of your eyes. You see how big I am, and what long sharp horns I have. Well, big as I am, and sharp as my horns are, yet Mr Man comes out and catches me. He puts me under a yoke, hitches me up in a cart, makes me haul his wood, and drives me anywhere he pleases. He does that. You had better let Mr Man alone. If you fool about with him, look out that he doesn't hitch

115

you up and have you prancing around here pulling his cart.'

"Mr Lion roared, and set out down the road. It was not very long before he came up with Mr Horse, who was nibbling and cropping the grass. Mr Lion made himself known, and asked Mr Horse if he knew Mr Man.

"'Very well indeed,' said Mr Horse; 'and more than that, I've known him for a very long time. What do you want with Mr Man?'

"'I'm hunting him up so as to thrash him,' said Mr Lion. 'They tell me that he is very stuck up, and I'm going to take him down a peg.'

"Mr Horse looked at Mr Lion as if he were sorry, and then he said:

"'I expect you had better let Mr Man alone. You see how big I am, how much strength I have, and how tough my feet are. Well, this Mr Man can take and hitch me up in his trap, and make me haul him all around. Then he can fasten me to the plough and make me break up all his new ground. You had better go back home. Before you know where you are, Mr Man will have you breaking up his new ground.'

"In spite of all this, Mr Lion shook his mane and said he was going to thrash Mr Man, anyhow. He went on down the big road, and presently he came up with Mr Jack Sparrow, sitting up in the top of the tree. Mr Jack Sparrow whirled around, and chirped, and fluttered, and apparently made a great fuss.

"'Hullo!' said he; 'who would have expected to see Mr Lion in this neighbourhood? Where are you going, Mr Lion?'

"Then Mr Lion asked Mr Jack Sparrow if he knew Mr Man, and Mr Jack Sparrow said that he knew Mr Man very well. Then Mr Lion asked Mr Jack Sparrow if he knew where he lived, and Mr Jack Sparrow said that he did. Mr Lion asked whereabouts he could find Mr Man, and Mr Jack Sparrow said he was across there in the new ground. He asked Mr Lion what he wanted with him, and Mr Lion responded that he was going to thrash Mr Man. With that Mr Jack Sparrow said:

"'You had better let Mr Man alone. You see how little I am, and how high I can fly; yet, in spite of that, Mr Man can bring me down when he wants to. You had better tuck up your tail and make for home, because Mr Man will bring you down.'

"But Mr Lion vowed that he would go after Mr Man. Go he would, and go he did. He had never seen Mr Man, and he didn't know what he looked like, but he went on toward the new ground. Sure enough, there was Mr Man splitting rails to make a fence. He was splitting away, when presently he heard a rustling in the bushes, and he looked up. There was Mr Lion. Mr Lion asked him if he knew Mr Man, and Mr Man declared that he knew him better than if he were his own twin-brother. Then Mr Lion said that he wanted to see him, and Mr Man said that if Mr Lion would come and stick his paw in the split so as to hold the log open till he came back, he would fetch Mr Man. Mr Lion marched up and put his paw in the place. Then Mr Man knocked out the wedge, and there Mr Lion was. Mr Man stood aside and said:

"'If you had been a steer or a horse, you might have run. If you had been a sparrow, you might have flown, but here you are, and you have caught yourself.'

"With that Mr Man strolled out into the bushes and cut a stick. He let out at Mr Lion and thrashed and thrashed him, until he could thrash him no more. And down to this day," continued Uncle Remus, in a tone calculated to destroy all doubt, "you can't get a lion to come up where there is a man splitting rails and put his paw in the split. That you can't."

XXXV

The Story of the Pigs

UNCLE REMUS relapsed into silence again, and the little boy, with nothing better to do, turned his attention to the bench upon which the old man kept his shoemaker's tools. Prosecuting his investigations in this direction, the youngster finally suggested that the supply of bristles was about exhausted.

"I don't know why Miss Sally wants to send you down here, if you are going to be fussing and bothering with those things," exclaimed Uncle Remus indignantly. "Now don't scatter those hog's bristles! The time was when it was very difficult to get bristle, and there is no telling when that time will come again. That's saying nothing of the time when the breed of hogs was run down to one poor little pig, and it seemed a very sorry business for those people who wanted bristle."

By this time Uncle Remus's indignation had vanished, disappearing as suddenly and unexpectedly as it came. The little boy was curious to know when and where and how the bristle famine occurred.

"I have already told you about that too long ago to talk about," the old man declared, but the little boy insisted that he had never heard about it before, and he was so persistent that at last Uncle Remus in self-defence consented to tell the story of the pigs.

"One time, away back yonder, the old Sow and all her children were living with the other creatures. I believe that the old Sow was a widow, and, if I am not mistaken, she had five children. Let me see," continued Uncle Remus, with the air of one determined to justify his memory by a reference to the record, and enumerating with great deliberation—"there was Big Pig, and there was Little Pig, and there was

Speckled Pig, and there was Blunt, and last of all there was Runt.

"One day the mother Pig knew that she was going to die, and she called all her children together to tell them that the time had come when they must look out for themselves. She told them also as well as she could, for her breath was very short, what a bad man old Brer Wolf was. She said that if they can keep out of the clutches of old Brer Wolf they will do very well indeed. Big Pig answered that she wasn't afraid. Blunt said that he was almost as big as Brer Wolf himself, while Runt just poked about in the straw and grunted. But the old widow Sow lay there and warned them that they had better keep their eyes on Brer Wolf, because he was a most mean and deceitful man.

"Not long after that, sure enough old Mrs Sow died, and all those children had to depend on themselves. So they set to work, and each one built a house to live in. Big Pig built a house of brush wood; Little Pig built a house of sticks; Speckled Pig built a house of mud; Blunt built a house of planks; and Runt didn't make any fuss or brag about what she was going to do, but she went to work and built a house of stone.

"By and by, when they had got everything finished, one morning old Brer Wolf came along, licking his chops and shaking his tail. The first house he came to was Big Pig's house. Brer Wolf walked up to the door and knocked softly—*blim! blim! blim!* There was no answer. Then he knocked loudly—*blam! blam! blam!* This woke up Big Pig, so she came to the door and asked who was that. Brer Wolf said it was a friend, and then he sang out:

"' *If you'll open the door and let me in,*
I 'll warm my hands and go home again.'

"Still Big Pig asked who it was, and then Brer Wolf said: 'How is your mother?'

"'My mother is dead,' said Big Pig, 'and before she died she told me to keep my eye on Brer Wolf. I see you through the crack of the door, and you look very like Brer Wolf.'

"Then old Brer Wolf drew a long breath as if he felt very ill, and he said:

"'I don't know what made your mother change so much, unless she was out of her mind. I heard that old Mrs Sow was sick, and I said to myself that I would call and see how the old lady was, and give her this bag of Indian corn. I know very well that if your mother were here now, and in her right mind, she would take the bag of corn and be glad to get it. More than that, she would ask me to sit by the fire and warm my hands.'

"The talk about the corn made Big Pig's mouth water, and after some more palaver she opened the door and let Brer Wolf in. Bless your heart, honey! that was the last of Big Pig. She had time neither to squeal nor even to grunt before Brer Wolf gobbled her up.

"The next day old Brer Wolf played the same trick on Little Pig. He went there and sang his song and Little Pig let him in. Then Brer Wolf returned the compliment by letting Little Pig in."

Here Uncle Remus laughed long and loud at his joke, and he took occasion to repeat it several times.

"Little Pig let Brer Wolf in, and Brer Wolf let Little Pig in, and what more can you ask than that? The next time Brer Wolf paid a call, he went to see Speckled Pig. He rapped at the door and sang his song:

> "'If you'll open the door and let me in,
> I'll warm my hands and go home again.'

"But Speckled Pig rather suspected something, and she refused to open the door. All the same Brer Wolf was a very deceitful man. He spoke in a voice that was both low and sweet. Presently he got his nose in the crack of the door, and he asked Speckled Pig just to let him get one paw in, and then he won't go any farther. He got the paw in, and then he begged to get the other paw in. When he got that he asked to get his head in, and when he got his head and his paws in, of course all that he had to do was to push open the door and walk in. When that was done, it wasn't long before he made fresh meat of Speckled Pig.

"The next day he did the same with Blunt, and the day after he declared that he would have a try for Runt. Now, that was exactly where old Brer Wolf made a mistake. He was like some other folk that I know. He would have been very smart if he hadn't been too smart. Runt was the littlest one of the whole family, yet all the same it was said that she had as much sense as grown-up folk.

"Brer Wolf crept up to Runt's house, and when he got underneath the window he sang:

"*'If you'll open the door and let me in,*
I'll warm my hands and go home again.'

"But, for all that, Brer Wolf couldn't coax Runt to open the door, and he couldn't break in because the house was built of stone. Presently Brer Wolf pretended that he had gone away, and then after a while he came back and knocked at the door—*blam! blam! blam!*

"Runt, who was sitting by the fire, scratched her ear and said:

"'Who is that?'

"'It's Speckled Pig,' said old Brer Wolf, in a tone that was between a snort and a grunt. 'I have brought you some peas for dinner.'

"Runt only laughed and replied:

"'Sis Speckled Pig never talked through so many teeth as that.'

"Brer Wolf went off again, and presently he came back and knocked. Runt sat and rocked herself and said:

"'Who is that?'

"'Big Pig,' said Brer Wolf. 'I have brought you some sweet corn for your supper.'

"Runt looked through the crack underneath the door, and laughed as she said:

"'Sis Big Pig hadn't any hair on her hoofs.'

"Then old Brer Wolf got mad and said that he would come down the chimney. Runt replied that it was the one and only way he could get it.

Then when she heard Brer Wolf climbing up on the outside of the chimney, she piled a whole lot of broomsage in front of the hearth, and when she heard him climbing down inside she took the tongs and put the straw on the fire. The smoke made Brer Wolf's head swim so much that he dropped down, and before he knew what was happening he was burnt to crackling. That was the last of old Brer Wolf. At least," added Uncle Remus, putting in a cautious proviso to fall back upon in case of an emergency, "at least it was the last of that Brer Wolf."

XXXVI

Mr Benjamin Ram and his Wonderful Fiddle

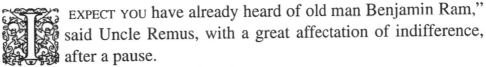I EXPECT YOU have already heard of old man Benjamin Ram," said Uncle Remus, with a great affectation of indifference, after a pause.

"Old man who?" asked the little boy.

"Old man Benjamin Ram. I expect you have heard all about him too long ago to talk about."

"Why, no, I haven't, Uncle Remus!" exclaimed the little boy, protesting and laughing. "He must have been a very funny old man."

"That's as may be," responded Uncle Remus sententiously. "What is fun in these days wouldn't have counted as fun in those days; and many a time I have seen folks laughing," continued the old man, with such withering sarcasm that the little boy immediately became serious—"many a time I have seen them laughing, when I'll be bound that they didn't know what they were laughing at themselves. And it isn't their laughing that annoys me either"—relenting a little—"it is this everlasting snickle and giggle, giggle and snickle."

Having thus mapped out, in a dim and uncertain way, what older people than the little boy might have been excused for accepting as a sort of moral basis, Uncle Remus proceeded:

"This Mr Benjamin Ram, who had just come into my mind, was a very old man. They tell me that he was one of those fiddlers who can't get the tune right unless they pat their foot. He was such a handy man to have at a merrymaking that the other creatures liked him immensely, and when they thought they would have a dance, a notion which struck them every now and then, nothing would do but that they must send for Mr Benjamin Ram. They say," continued Uncle Remus, closing his eyes in a sort of ecstasy, "that when he squared himself back in a chair, and fairly got going, he could give those old-time tunes as they were in the very beginning. And when the dance was done all the creatures would set to and help fill a bag of peas for old Mr Benjamin Ram to take home with him.

"At one time, just about Christmas, Miss Meadows and Miss Motts and the girls made up their minds that they would give a party, and they sent word to old man Benjamin Ram that they expected him to be there. When the time came for Mr Benjamin Ram to start, the wind blew cold and the clouds began to spread across the sky—but that made no difference; old man Benjamin Ram took down his walking-stick, tied up his fiddle in a bag, and set out for Miss Meadows. He thought he knew the way, but it got colder and colder, and more cloudy, till presently Mr Benjamin Ram had quite lost his way. If he had kept on down the big road from the start, it might have been different, but he took a short cut, and he hadn't gone far before he was lost sure enough. He went this way and that way and the other way, but all the same he was quite lost. Some people would have sat down just where they were and thought out the way, but old man Benjamin Ram hadn't got a wrinkle on his horn for nothing. He had been given the name of old Billy Hardhead long before that. Then again, some folks would have stopped still and shouted and bawled to see if they couldn't rouse some of the neighbours, but old Mr Benjamin Ram faced the wind, and marched right on just as if he knew that he wasn't going the wrong way. He kept on, but before long he began to feel very lonely, especially when he thought how Miss Meadows and the girls and all the company would be obliged to do the best they could without any fiddling. It sent a shiver down his back when he remembered that he would have to sleep out there in the woods by himself.

"Nevertheless, he kept on till it began to get dark. Then he still kept on until by and by he came to a little rise where there was a clay patch. When he got there he stopped and looked around. Away down in the hollow he saw a light shining. When he saw this, old man Benjamin Ram put his best foot foremost, and made for it as if it was the very place for which he had been looking. It wasn't long before he came to the house where the light was, and, bless your heart, he didn't hesitate to knock. Then somebody said:

"'Who is that?'

"'I'm Mr Benjamin Ram, and I have quite lost my way. I have come to ask you if you can take me in for the night.'

"As a rule," continued Uncle Remus, "old Mr Benjamin Ram was very rough and ready in the way he spoke, but you may believe that he was most polite in his talk this time.

"Then some one on the other side of the door asked Mr Benjamin Ram to walk in, and with that he opened the door and walked in, making a bow as fiddling folks do when they go in company. He had no sooner made his bow and looked around, however, before he began to shake and to shiver as if he had been stricken with the ague, because sitting right there before the fire was old Brer Wolf, with his teeth showing up all white and shiny as if they were brand new. If Mr Benjamin Ram hadn't been so old and stiff I warrant you he would have turned and run away, but almost before he had time to think, old Brer Wolf had jumped up, shut the door, and fastened it with a great big chain. Old Mr Benjamin Ram knew that he was in for it, so he put on the boldest face that he was able, but you may be sure that he just longed to be lost in the woods again. Then he made another low bow, and said that he hoped Brer Wolf and all his family were well. He had dropped in, he said, to warm himself and to inquire the way to Miss Meadows's. If Brer Wolf would be so good as to set him in his road again, he would be going pretty soon and he would be much obliged into the bargain.

"'To be sure, Mr Ram,' said Brer Wolf, while he licked his chops and grinned; 'just put your walking-stick in the corner, and set your bag on the floor, and make yourself at home. We haven't got much, but what we have is yours while you stay, and I'll be bound that we will take good care of you.' With that Brer Wolf laughed and showed his teeth so much that old man Benjamin Ram came very near having another attack of ague.

"Then Brer Wolf flung another log on the fire, and slipped into the back room. Presently, while old Mr Benjamin Ram was sitting there shaking in his shoes, he heard Brer Wolf whispering to his wife:

"'Wife! Wife! Fling away your smoked meat—fresh meat for supper! Fling away your smoked meat—fresh meat for supper!'

"Then old Mrs Wolf talked out loud so that Mr Benjamin Ram could hear:

"'To be sure I'll get him some supper. We are away off here in the woods, so far from company that goodness knows I'm very glad to see Mr Benjamin Ram.'

"Then Mr Benjamin Ram heard old Mrs Wolf whetting her knife on a rock—*shirrah! shirrah! shirrah!*—and every time he heard that knife say *shirrah!* he knew he was that much nearer to the dinner-pot. He knew that he couldn't get away, and while he sat there thinking it struck him that he might as well play one more tune on his fiddle before the worst came to the worst. With that he untied that bag and took out the fiddle and began to tune up-*plink, plank, plunk, plink! plunk, plank, plink, plunk!*"

Uncle Remus's imitation of the tuning of a fiddle was marvellous enough to produce a startling effect upon a much less enthusiastic listener than the little boy. It was given in perfect good faith, but the serious expression on the old man's face was so irresistibly comic that the child laughed until the tears ran down his face. Uncle Remus very properly accepted this as a tribute to his wonderful resources as a story-teller, and continued, in great good-humour:

"When old Mrs Wolf heard that sound, of course she wondered what it was, and dropped her knife to listen. Old Mr Benjamin Ram didn't know this, and he kept on tuning up—*plank, plink, plunk, plank!* Then old Mrs Wolf nudged Brer Wolf with her elbow, and said:

"'Hullo, old man, what's that?'

"Then both of them pricked up their ears and listened, and just then old Mr Benjamin Ram fixed the fiddle under his chin and struck up one of those old-time tunes."

"Well, what tune was it, Uncle Remus?" the little boy asked, with some display of impatience.

"Bless me if I haven't quite forgotten that tune," continued Uncle Remus; "it went something like that song about 'Sheep shell corn with the rattle of his horn,' and then it might have been that one about 'Roll the key, ladies, roll those keys.' Brer Wolf and old Mrs Wolf listened and listened, and the more they listened the more frightened they got, until by and by they took to their heels and ran for the swamp at the back of the house as if the police were after them.

"When old Mr Benjamin Ram had finished his fiddling, he didn't see Brer Wolf and he couldn't hear old Mrs Wolf. Then he looked in the back room; no Wolf there. Then he looked in the back porch; no Wolf there. Then he looked in the cupboard, no Wolf there either. Then old Mr Benjamin Ram shut all the doors and locked them. After that he searched around and found in the loft some peas and fodder, which he had for his supper. Then he lay down before the fire and slept as soundly as a log.

"Next morning he was up and stirring very early. He put out from there and he found the way to Miss Meadows's house in time to play at the party. When he got there, Miss Meadows and the girls ran to the gate to meet him. This one took his hat, that one took his stick, the other one took his fiddle, and they all said:

"'Law, Mr Ram! where in the name of goodness have you been? We are so glad you have come. Bustle around, everybody, and get Mr Ram a cup of hot coffee.'

"They made a big fuss of Mr Benjamin Ram, Miss Meadows and Miss Motts and the girls did, but between you and me and the bed-post, honey, they would have had their dance whether the old chap had been there or not, because the girls had made arrangements with Brer Rabbit to pat for them, and in those days Brer Rabbit was a patter indeed, man. He most surely was."

XXXVII

BRER RABBIT'S RIDDLE

OULD BRER RABBIT pat a tune, sure enough, Uncle Remus?" asked the little boy, his thoughts apparently dwelling upon the new accomplishment of Brer Rabbit at which the old man had hinted in his story of Mr Benjamin Ram. Uncle Remus pretended to be greatly surprised that anyone could be so unfamiliar with the accomplishments of Brer Rabbit as to venture to ask such a question. His response was in the nature of a comment:

"Goodness me! what kind of pass is this we are coming to when a great big grown-up youngster asks such a question about Brer Rabbit? Bless your heart, honey! there was no tune going that Brer Rabbit could not pat. Not only that, when there was somebody else to do the patting, Brer Rabbit could jump out into the middle of the floor and actually shake the eyelids off of the other creatures. And it wasn't any of this bowing and scraping and slipping and sliding, and hands all around, which folks do in these days. It was this up and down kind of dancing where they just jump up in the air to cut the pigeon-wing, and alight on the floor right in the middle of the double-shuffle. *Shoo!* There isn't any dancing in these days; folks' shoes are too light, and they aren't so nimble as they used to be. That they aren't.

"And yet," Uncle Remus continued, in a tone which seemed to imply that he deemed it necessary to apologize for the apparent frivolity of Brer Rabbit —"and yet the time came when old Brer Rabbit began to put this and that together, and the notion struck him that he had better be at home looking after the interests of his family, instead of gadding about to all the merrymakings in the settlement He thought this over until presently he set out, determined that he would earn his own living. Then he set to work to lay off a piece of ground and plant a potato-patch for himself.

"Brer Fox saw all this going on, and declared to himself that he expected Brer Rabbit was frightened and had lost all his rashness. So he made up his mind that he would pay back Brer Rabbit for all his deceitfulness. He started, and from that time on he worried Brer Rabbit about his potato-patch. One night he left the draw-board down, another night he flung off the top of the railings, and the next night he tore down a part of the fence, and he kept on in this way until apparently Brer Rabbit didn't know what to do. All this time Brer Fox kept on fooling with the potato-patch, and when he saw that Brer Rabbit wasn't making any motion, Brer Fox thought that he was frightened sure enough, and that the time had come to gobble him up without leave or licence. So he called on Brer Rabbit and asked him if he would take a walk. Brer Rabbit asked where. Brer Fox said, right out yonder. Brer Rabbit asked him what there was right out yonder. Brer Fox said he knew where were some very fine peaches and he wanted Brer Rabbit to go along and climb the tree and fling them down. Brer Rabbit said that he didn't care if he did, especially to oblige Brer Fox.

"They set out, and after a while, sure enough, they came to a peach-orchard. Brer Rabbit picked out a good tree, and up he climbed. Brer Fox sat at the root of the tree, because he thought that when Brer Rabbit came down he would have to down backward, and that would be just the time to nab him. But, bless your heart, honey, Brer Rabbit saw what Brer Fox was after before he climbed up. When he picked the peaches, Brer Fox said:

"'Fling them down, Brer Rabbit—fling them down so that I can catch them.'

"Brer Rabbit winked the eye that was away from Brer Fox, and shouted back:

"'If I fling them down where you are, Brer Fox, and you miss them, they will get squashed, so I'll throw them out in the grass where they won't burst.'

"Then he flung the peaches out in the grass, and while Brer Fox went after them he came down out of the tree, and hustled until he had elbow-room. When he got a little way away, he shouted back to Brer Fox that he had a riddle which he wanted him to read. Brer Fox asked what it was. With that, Brer Rabbit gave it out to Brer Fox like a man making a speech:

> "'The big bird rob and the little bird sing,
> The big bee hum and the little bee sting,
> The little man lead and the big horse follow—
> Can you tell me what's good for a head in a hollow?'

"Old Brer Fox scratched his head and thought, and thought and scratched his head, but the more he thought the worse he got mixed up with the riddle, and after a while he had to tell Brer Rabbit that he couldn't for the life of him tell how to unriddle that riddle.

"'Come along with me,' said old Brer Rabbit, 'and I'll show you how to read that riddle. It's one of those riddles,' said old man Rabbit, 'which before you read them you have to eat a morsel of honey, and I know the place where we can get some honey.'

"Brer Fox asked whereabouts it was, and Brer Rabbit said it was up there in old Brer Bear's cotton-patch, where he had several bee-gums. Brer Fox said he hadn't much of a sweet-tooth, yet he did want to get at the meaning of that riddle, so that he didn't care if he came with him.

"They set out, and it wasn't long before they came to old Brer Bear's bee-gums. Old Brer Rabbit gave them a rap with his walking-stick, just as folks rap water-melons to see if they are ripe. He tapped and he rapped, until he came to one which sounded as if it was full. Then he went behind it, and said:

"'I'll just tilt it, Brer Fox, and you can put your head underneath it and get some of the drippings.'

"Brer Rabbit tilted it, and, sure enough, Brer Fox put his head underneath. It makes me laugh," continued Uncle Remus, with a chuckle, "to think how simple Brer Fox was, because no sooner had he stuck his head underneath that bee-gum than Brer Rabbit tipped it right over, and down it came—*ker-swosh!*—right on Brer Fox's neck, and there he was. Brer Fox kicked and squealed and jumped and squalled and danced and pranced and begged and prayed, yet there he was. And when Brer Rabbit got some distance off, he turned around to look back, and saw Brer Fox wriggling and squirming. Right then and there Brer Rabbit gave an old-time war-whoop and put out for home.

"When he got there, the first man he saw was Brer Fox's grandfather, whom folks all call Grandsire Grey Fox. When Brer Rabbit saw him, he said:

"'How are you, Grandsire Grey Fox?'

"'I still keep poorly, thank you, Brer Rabbit,' said Grandsire Grey Fox. 'Have you seen anything of my grandson this morning?'

"With that Brer Rabbit laughed, and said that he and Brer Fox had been rambling around together and having more fun than a man could shake a stick at.

"'We've been making riddles and reading them,' said Brer Rabbit. 'Brer Fox is sitting somewhere in the bushes now, trying to read one that I gave him. I'll just give you one, and if you can read it, it will take you to the very spot where your grandson is, and you can't get there too soon.'

"Then old Grandsire Grey Fox asked what it was, and Brer Rabbit sang:

"'*The big bird rob and the little bird sing,*
The big bee hum and the little bee sting,
The little man lead and the big horse follow—
Can you tell me what's good for a head in a hollow?'

"Grandsire Grey Fox took a pinch of snuff, gave a little cough, and thought and thought, but he couldn't make it out, so Brer Rabbit laughed and sang:

"'Bee-gum very big to make the Fox a collar,
Can you tell me what's good for a head in a hollow?'

"After some time, Grandsire Grey Fox began to catch a glimpse of what Brer Rabbit was trying to tell him, so he wished Brer Rabbit good day, and shuffled off to find his grandson."

"And did he find him, Uncle Remus?" asked the little boy.

"To be sure, honey. Brer Bear heard the hubbub that Brer Fox was making, and he went down to see what was the matter. As soon as he saw how the land lay, of course he got the idea that Brer Fox had been robbing the bee-gums. So he got a handful of sticks, Brer Bear did, and let out at Brer Fox, warming his jacket in good style. Then he let him go, but it wasn't long before all the neighbours got word that Brer Fox had been robbing Brer Bear's bee-gums."

XXXVIII

How Mr Rooster lost his Dinner

I	T SEEMED that the rainy season had set in in earnest, but the little boy went down to Uncle Remus's cabin before dark. In some mysterious way, it appeared to the child, the gloom of twilight fastened itself upon the dusky clouds, and the great trees without, and the dismal perspective beyond, gradually became one with the darkness. Uncle Remus had thoughtfully placed a tin pan under a leak in the roof, and the *drip-drip-drip* of the water, as it fell in the resonant vessel, made a not unmusical accompaniment to the storm.

The old man fumbled around under his bed, and presently dragged forth a large bag filled with light-wood knots, which, with an instinctive economy in this particular direction, he had stored away for an emergency. A bright but flickering flame was the result of this timely discovery, and the effect it produced was quite in keeping with all the surroundings. The rain, and wind, and darkness held sway without, while within, the unsteady light-wood blaze seemed to rime with the *drip-drip-drip* in the pan. Sometimes the shadow of Uncle Remus, as he leaned over the hearth, would tower and fill the cabin, and again it would fade and disappear among the swaying and swinging cobwebs that curtained the rafters.

"When bed-time comes, honey," said Uncle Remus in a soothing tone, "I'll just take down your father's carriage umbrella from the corner as I have been doing. Then I'll take you under my arm and set you down on Miss Sally's hearth just as dry and as warm as a rat's nest inside a haystack."

At this juncture 'Tildy, the house-girl, rushed in out of the rain and darkness with a waterproof cloak and an umbrella, and announced her mission to the little boy without taking time to catch her breath.

"Miss Sally says that you have to come back at once," she exclaimed, "because she's afraid that lightning may strike some of these high trees."

Uncle Remus rose from his stooping posture in front of the hearth and assumed a threatening attitude.

"Well, did anybody ever hear anything to beat that!" was his indignant exclamation. "Look here, girl, don't you try to play the fool with me—don't you do it. Because if you do, I'll just give you a clip that will put you to bed before bed-time comes. That's what."

"Bless me! what have I gone and done to Uncle Remus now?" asked 'Tildy, with a great affectation of innocent ignorance.

"I'm going to put on my coat and take that umbrella, and I'm going straight up to the big house to ask Miss Sally if she sent you down with any such message, when she knew that the child was sitting here with me. I'm going to ask her," continued Uncle Remus, "and if she hasn't sent such a message, then I'm going to fetch myself back. Now, you just watch what I do."

"Well, I heard Miss Sally say that she was afraid that lightning might strike the place somewhere," said 'Tildy, in a tone which manifested her willingness to compromise all differences, "and then I asked her if I could come down here, and she said that I had better bring this cloak and parasol."

"Now that you have brought them," responded Uncle Remus, "you had better put them in that chair and take yourself off. Thunder is very likely to hit close to where these slick-headed folks are."

But the little boy finally prevailed on the old man to allow 'Tildy to remain, and after a while he put matters on a peace footing by inquiring if roosters crowed at night when it was raining.

"That they do," responded Uncle Remus. "Wet or dry, they flap their wings and wake up all the neighbours. Lord bless my soul!" he exclaimed suddenly, "whatever made me forget Mr Rooster?"

"What about him?" inquired the little boy.

"At one time," said Uncle Remus, knocking the ashes off his hands and knees, "there were two plantations side by side, and on both of these plantations there were a lot of fowls. They were most sociable in those days, and it turned out that the fowls on one plantation gave a party for which they sent out invitations to the fowls on the other plantations.

"When the day came, Mr Rooster blew his horn and assembled them all, and after they had assembled they got in line. Mr Rooster took the lead, and after him came old lady Hen and Miss Pullet, and then there was Mr Peafowl, Mr Turkey Gobbler, Miss Guinea Hen, Miss Puddle Duck, and all the rest of them. They started off in a rather ragged fashion, but it wasn't long before they all caught the step, and then they marched down by the spring, up through the horse-lot, and across by the ginhouse, and it wasn't long before they got to the place where the party was.

"They danced and they played and they sang. Especially they played and sang that song which ran like this:

"'*Come under, come under,*
My honey, my love, my own true love;
My heart's been a weeping
Way down in Galilee.'

"They were going on in this way, having their amusements, when, by and by, old Mr Peafowl got on the roof of the barn and blew the dinner-horn. They all washed their faces and hands in the back porch, and then they went in to dinner. When they got there they saw nothing but a pile of corn-bread. Loaves were piled on loaves, and on the top of all was a great big ash-cake. Mr Rooster looked at this and turned up his nose, and after a while strutted out. Old Miss Guinea Hen was watching Mr Rooster's movements, and when she saw this she squalled:

"'*Pot-rack! Pot-rack!* Mr Rooster gone back! *Pot-rack! Pot-rack!*

Mr Rooster gone back!'

"With that they all made a great fuss. Miss Hen and Miss Pullet cackled and squalled; Mr Gobbler gobbled, and Miss Puddle Duck shook her tail and said, '*Quickity-quack-quack*.' But Mr Rooster ruffled up his cape and marched out.

"This rather put a damper on the others, but before Mr Rooster got out of sight and hearing they set to work on the pile that appeared to be nothing but corn-bread, and, lo and behold, underneath the loaves of bread were meat and greens, baked potatoes, and boiled turnips. Mr Rooster heard the ladies making a great fuss, so he stopped to look through the crack in the door. There he could see all the doings and arrangements. He felt as if he had been had when he saw all this, and the other fowls shouted to him and asked him to come back. His crop, which was very empty, also asked him to go back, but he was very big and stuck up, so he strutted off, crowing as he went. But his experience that time has lasted him and all his family down to this very day. And you needn't take my word for it either, because if you will just keep your eye open and watch, you will catch a glimpse of old Mr Rooster's folks scratching where-ever they expect to find their food. More than that, they will scratch with their food in full sight. Since that time none of the Roosters have been fooled by what they have seen on top. They haven't rested until they have seen what has been underneath. They will scratch in spite of all creation."

"That's the Lord's truth!" said 'Tildy, with unction. "I've seen them with my own eyes. That I have."

This was 'Tildy's method of renewing peaceful relations with Uncle Remus, but the old man was disposed to resist the attempt.

"You would be better up yonder washing the dishes, instead of coming down here with tales that Miss Sally never dreamt of saying."

XXXIX

BRER RABBIT BREAKS UP A PARTY

As LONG AS Uncle Remus allowed 'Tildy to remain in the cabin, the little boy was not particularly interested in preventing the perfunctory abuse which the old man might feel disposed to bestow upon the complacent girl. The truth is, the child's mind was occupied with the episode in the story of Mr Benjamin Ram which treats of the style in which this romantic old wag put Mr and Mrs Wolf to flight by playing a tune upon his fiddle. The little boy was particularly struck with this remarkable feat, and he made bold to recur to it again by asking Uncle Remus for all the details. It was plain to the latter that the child regarded Mr Ram as the typical hero of all the animals, and this was by no means gratifying to the old man. He answered the questions as well as he could, and, when nothing more remained to be said about Mr Ram, he settled himself back in his chair and resumed the curious history of Brer Rabbit.

"Of course Mr Ram was a very clever man. I am not going to dispute that; but neither Mr Ram nor Mr Lam were equal to Brer Rabbit. Mr Benjamin Ram frightened away Brer Wolf and his wife with his fiddle, but, bless your heart, old Brer Rabbit did much more than that."

"What did Brer Rabbit do?" asked the little boy.

"At one time," said Uncle Remus, "Brer Fox asked some of the other creatures to come to his house. He asked Brer Bear, and Brer Wolf, and Brer Coon, but he- didn't ask Brer Rabbit. All the same, Brer Rabbit got wind of it, and he declared that if he didn't go, he expected that he would have as much fun as the next man.

"The creatures who were invited assembled at Brer Fox's house, and Brer Fox asked them in and got them some chairs. There they sat, laughing and talking, until presently Brer Fox fetched out a bottle and put it on the sideboard. Then he stepped back and said:

"'Just step up, gentlemen, and help yourselves,' and you may well believe that they did help themselves.

"While this drinking was going on, what do you think Brer Rabbit was doing? You may be sure that Brer Rabbit was extremely busy, because he was in the neighbourhood making his arrangements. A long time before that, Brer Rabbit had been at a party, and while all the folks were down at the spring eating dinner, Brer Rabbit crept up and ran off with one of the drums. There was a big drum and a little drum, and Brer Rabbit snatched up the little one and ran home.

"Now then, when he heard about the other creatures going to Brer Fox's house, what did Brer Rabbit do but get out this rattling drum, and go down the road toward the place where they were. He took that drum," continued Uncle Remus with great elation of voice and manner, "and he went down the road toward Brer Fox's house, and he made the drum talk like thunder mixed with hail. It talked in this way:

"*Diddybum, diddybum, diddybum-bum-bum—diddybum!*

"The other creatures were drinking, and drinking, and going on a terrible rate, so that they didn't hear the noise, but all the same, there came Brer Rabbit:

"*Diddybum, diddybum, diddybum-bum-bum—diddybum!*

"Presently Brer Coon, who always had one ear hanging out for the news, asked Brer Fox what was that, and by that time all the creatures stopped and listened; but all the same, there came Brer Rabbit:

"*Diddybum, diddybum, diddybum-bum-bum—diddybum!*

"The creatures kept on listening, and Brer Rabbit kept on getting nearer, until by and by Brer Coon reached under the chair for his hat, and said:

"'Well, gentlemen, I expect I had better be going. I told my wife that I wouldn't be gone a minute, and here's the evening coming on.'

"With that Brer Coon skipped off, but he hadn't got much farther than the back gate before there came all the other creatures, just as if they were running a race, and old Brer Fox was trying to get the lead."

"There now," exclaimed 'Tildy, with great fervour.

"Yes, there they were, and there they went," continued Uncle Remus. "They took short cuts; they scrambled over one another; and they didn't rest until they got in the bushes.

"Old Brer Rabbit came on down the road—*diddybum, diddybum, diddybum-bum-bum*—and goodness me! when he got to Brer Fox's house there was nobody there. Brer Rabbit was that daring that he hunted all around until he found an air-hole in the drum. When he put his mouth to it and sang out:

"'Is there anybody home?' and then he answered himself, 'Why, no, honey, the folks are all gone.'

"With that, old Brer Rabbit broke loose and laughed fit to kill himself. Then he opened wide Brer Fox's front gate, and marched up to the house. When he got there he opened the door and called Brer Fox; but nobody was there. So Brer Rabbit walked in and took a chair and made himself at home.

"Brer Rabbit hadn't sat there long before he caught a whiff of the drink—"

"You hear that?" exclaimed 'Tildy with convulsive admiration.

"He caught a whiff of that drink, and then he saw it on the sideboard; so he stepped up, and poured a tumblerful down in the direction of his throat. Brer Rabbit was very like some other people I know. He took one tumblerful, and it wasn't long before he took another, and when a man goes on in this way," continued Uncle Remus, somewhat apologetically, he is bound to show the effects of it."

"Truth, too!" said 'Tildy, by way of hearty confirmation.

"All this time the other creatures were down in the bushes listening for the *diddybum*, and preparing to run away from there at the slightest warning. But as they heard nothing more, Brer Fox said that he was going back to look after the goods, and the other creatures said that they believed that they would go with him. They started out, and crept toward Brer Fox's house, but they crept very carefully, and I'll be bound that if somebody had just shaken a bush, those creatures would have torn up the earth in their haste to get away from there. But still there was no noise, so they kept on creeping until they got in the house.

"When they got there, the first sight they saw was old Brer Rabbit standing up by the drambottle mixing himself a toddy, and he wasn't very sure on his legs either, because he was swaying from side to side, and he looked pretty limp, as you might expect him to be after drinking the kind of liquor which Brer Fox had provided for those creatures.

"When Brer Fox saw Brer Rabbit making free with his belongings in that way, what do you think he did?" inquired Uncle Remus, with the air of one seeking general information.

"I expect he cussed," said 'Tildy, who was apt to take a vividly practical view of matters.

"He was glad," said the little boy, "because he had a good chance to catch Brer Rabbit."

"To be sure he was," continued Uncle Remus, heartily assenting to the child's interpretation of the situation; "to be sure he was. He stood there, Brer Fox did, and watched Brer Rabbit's motions. By and by he shouted:

"'Aye, aye! Brer Rabbit,' says he. 'Many a time you have made your escape, but now I've got you!'

"And with that Brer Fox and the other creatures closed in on Brer Rabbit.

"I think I told you that Brer Rabbit had taken more drink than was good for him. Yet his head didn't swim so much but he could tell what he was doing, and by the time that he set eyes on Brer Fox he knew that he had got in close quarters. As soon as he saw this, Brer Rabbit made as if he had been drinking more than he really had, and he staggered about like a town-girl in a flat-bottomed boat, and seemed as if he were as limp as a wet rag. He staggered up to Brer Fox, rolled his eyes, and, slapping him on the back, asked him how his mother was.

Then when he saw the other creatures," continued Uncle Remus, "he talked so strangely that they had no end of fun. By and by, however, Brer Fox said that they had better get to business. Then they all closed in on Brer Rabbit, and there he was.

"In those days old Brer Bear was a judge among the creatures, and they all asked him what they were going to do with Brer Rabbit. Judge Bear put on his spectacles, cleared his throat, and said that the best thing to do with a man who had made such a noise, and made the neighbours run out of their own house, and had made free with the pantry, was to drown him. Then old Brer Fox clapped his hands, and said that he believed that Judge Bear had read all the law-books, because that was exactly what they said ought to be done to a man who made free with his neighbours' pantry.

"Then Brer Rabbit pretended that he was frightened, and he cried, begging them in the name of goodness not to fling him in the stream, because they knew that he didn't know how to swim; but if they were obliged to pitch him in, for mercy's sake to get a walking-stick, so that he could have something to hold on to while he was drowning.

"Old Brer Bear scratched his head and said that, as far as his remembrance went, there was nothing against that in the law-books, so they all agreed that Brer Rabbit should have a walking-stick.

"With that, they caught up Brer Rabbit, put him on a wheel-barrow, and carried him down to the stream, and flung him in."

"Eh-eh!" exclaimed 'Tildy, with well-feigned astonishment.

"They flung him in," continued Uncle Remus, "and Brer Rabbit alighted on his feet, the same as a tom-cat, and picked his way out by the help of the walking-stick. The water was so shallow that it only came over Brer Rabbit's slipper, and when he got out at the other side he shouted back:

"'So long, Brer Fox!'"

XL

Brer Tarrypin Deceives Brer Buzzard

HERE WAS a pause here, which was finally broken by 'Tildy, whose remark was in the nature of a very undignified yawn. Uncle Remus regarded her for a moment with an expression of undisguised scorn, which quickly expressed itself in words:

"If you had been out of the house then, you would have taken us all in. It is a pity there isn't some place or other where these girls can go to learn manners."

'Tildy, however, ignored the old man, and, with a toss of her head, said to the little boy in a cool, exasperating tone, employing a pet name she had heard the child's mother use:

"Well, Pinx, I expect we had better be going. The rain is nearly over now, and presently the stars will be shining. Miss Sally is looking for you now this minute."

"You had better go wherever you are going, you trifling huzzy, you!" exclaimed Uncle Remus. "You had better go and get your Jim Crow card and straighten out those kinks in your hair. I always hear white folks say that you had better keep your eye on those who have got their hair done up in strings. Now I give you fair warning."

"Uncle Remus," said the little boy, when the old man's wrath had somewhat subsided, "why do they call them Jim Crow cards?"

"I'll be blessed if I know, honey, except that it's the one and only machine which certain folks can uncomb their kinks with. Now, then," continued the old man, straightening up and speaking with considerable animation, "that reminds me about a riddle that has been running round in my head. And that riddle it's the hardest riddle that I ever heard. It goes like this: If he comes, he doesn't come; if he doesn't come, he comes. Now I'll be bound you can't tell me what that is."

After some time spent in vain guessing, the little boy confessed that he did not know.

"It's crow and corn," said Uncle Remus sententiously.

"Crow and corn, Uncle Remus?"

"Of course, honey. Crow comes, and corn doesn't come; crow doesn't come, and then the corn comes."

"That's so," said 'Tildy "I've seen them pull up corn, and I've seen corn grow which they haven't pulled up."

If 'Tildy thought to propitiate Uncle Remus, she was mistaken. He scowled at her, and addressed himself to the little boy:

"The crow was a near relative of the buzzard, and that reminds me that we haven't kept in touck with old Brer Buzzard as we should have done.

"Whatever might be the case in these days, I'm not saying, but in those times old Brer Tarrypin loved honey even more than Brer Bear. He was so flat-footed, however, that when he found a beetree he couldn't climb it, and he went so slowly that he could hardly find one. One day, when he was down the road, just longing for some honey, whom should he meet but Brer Buzzard.

"They shook hands in a very friendly way, and asked about the news of the neighbourhood. Then after a while Brer Tarrypin said to Brer Buzzard that he wanted to go into partnership with him for getting honey, and it wasn't long before they struck an agreement. Brer Buzzard was to fly around and look for the bee-tree, and Brer Tarrypin was to creep and crawl and hunt on the ground.

"They started out, old Brer Buzzard sailing around in the elements, and old Brer Tarrypin shuffling and shambling on the ground. In almost the very first field he came to Brer Tarrypin struck up with a great big bumble-bees' nest in the ground. He looked around, then he thrust in his head and tasted the honey, and then he pulled it out again and looked all around to see if he could catch a glimpse of Brer Buzzard. But Brer Buzzard didn't seem to be anywhere in sight. Then Brer Tarrypin said to himself that he expected that that bumblebee honey wasn't the kind of honey that they had been talking about, and, anyway, there wasn't very much honey there. With that, Brer Tarrypin crept into the hole and gobbled up the last drop of the bumble-bee honey by himself. After he had finished, he came out and made haste to lick it all off his feet, so that Brer Buzzard wouldn't be able to see that he had got some honey.

"Then old Brer Tarrypin stretched out his neck and tried to lick the honey from his back, but his neck was too short. He tried to scrape it off against a tree, but it wouldn't come off. Then he rolled on the ground, but still it didn't come off. Then old Brer Tarrypin jumped up, and said that he would make his way home, and that when Brer Buzzard came he would lie on his back and say that he was sick, and so Brer Buzzard wouldn't be able to see the honey.

"Brer Tarrypin started off, but when he happened to look up, lo and behold, there was Brer Buzzard hovering right over the very spot where he was. Brer Tarrypin knew that Brer Buzzard would be sure to see him if he started off home. More than that, he knew that he would find him out if he didn't stir himself and do something very quickly. With that, Brer Tarrypin shuffled back to the bumble-bees' nest as fast as he could, lit a fire there, and then crawled back, shouting:

"'Brer Buzzard! O Brer Buzzard! Run here, for goodness sake, Brer Buzzard, and see how much honey I have found! I just crept in a little way, and it dripped all down my back like water. Run here, Brer Buzzard! Half is yours and half mine, Brer Buzzard!'

"Brer Buzzard flopped down, laughing and saying that he was very glad because he had got terribly hungry up where he had been. Then Brer Tarrypin told Brer Buzzard to creep in a little way, and taste and see how he liked it, while he would take his stand outside and watch. But no sooner did Brer Buzzard creep in the bumble-bees' nest than Brer Tarrypin rolled a great big rock in front of the hole. Directly, the fire began to burn Brer Buzzard, and he sang out like a man in trouble:

"'Something is biting me, Brer Tarrypin—something is biting me, Brer Tarrypin!'

"Then old Brer Tarrypin shouted back:

"'It's the bumble-bees stinging you, Brer Buzzard; stand up and flap your wings, Brer Buzzard. Stand up and flap your wings, Brer Buzzard, and you'll drive them off.'

"Brer Buzzard flapped and flapped his wings, but the more he flapped, the more he fanned the fire, and it wasn't long before he was burnt right up, all except the big end of his wing-feathers, and those old Brer Tarrypin made into some quills, on which he went around playing, and the tune he played was this:

> *"'I foolee, I foolee, I foolee poor Buzzard;*
> *Poor Buzzard, I foolee. I foolee, I foolee.'"*

XLI

BRER FOX COVETS THE QUILLS

"T HAT MUST have been a mighty funny song," said the little boy. "What is fun one time isn't fun at another; some folks find fun where others find trouble. Yet, fun or no fun, that was the Song which Brer Tarrypin played on the quills:

> "'I foolee, I foolee, I foolee poor Buzzard;
> Poor Buzzard, I foolee, I foolee, I foolee.'

"Nobody knew where the quills came from, because Brer Tarrypin wasn't bragging about how he got them. Yet everybody wanted them on account of their playing such a thrilling tune, and old Brer Fox wanted them most of all. He begged and begged Brer Tarrypin to sell him those quills; but Brer Tarrypin held on tight, and said eh-eh! Then he asked Brer Tarrypin to lend them to him just for a week, so that he could play them to his children; but Brer Tarrypin shook his head, and put his foot down and kept on playing:

> "'I foolee, I foolee, I foolee poor Buzzard;
> Poor Buzzard, I foolee, I foolee, I foolee.'

"But Brer Fox had no peace of mind on account, of those quills. One day he met Brer Tarrypin and asked him how he and his family and all his children were getting on. Then he asked him if he couldn't just look at these quills, because he had some goose-feathers at home, and if he could just get a glimpse of Brer Tarrypin's quills, he thought he could make some very like them.

"Brer Tarrypin thought about this, but he hated to deny any small favours like that, so by and by he held out the quills where Brer Fox could see them. With that, Brer Fox jerked the quills out of Brer Tarrypin's hand, and dashed off just as hard as he could go. Brer Tarrypin shouted and shouted after him as loud as he could shout, but he knew that he couldn't catch him, so he sat there, Brer Tarrypin did, and looked as if he had lost all the friends he had in the round world.

"After this Brer Fox strutted around and played in a very large way, and every time he met Brer Tarrypin in the road he walked all round him and played on the quills like this:

> *" 'I foolee, I foolee poor Buzzard;*
> *I foolee old Tarrypin too.'*

"Brer Tarrypin felt very uneasy, but he didn't say anything. At last, one day while old Brer Tarrypin was sitting on a log sunning himself, there came Brer Fox playing that same old tune on the quills, but Brer Tarrypin stayed still. Brer Fox came a little nearer and played, but Brer Tarrypin kept his eyes shut and stayed still. Brer Fox came nearer and got on the log; Brer Tarrypin said nothing. Brer Fox got still nearer and played on the quills, still Brer Tarrypin said nothing.

"'Brer Tarrypin is very sleepy this morning,' said Brer Fox.

"Still Brer Tarrypin kept his eyes shut and stayed still. Brer Fox kept on getting nearer and nearer, until Brer Tarrypin opened his eyes and his mouth at the same time, made a grab at Brer Fox, and missed him.

"But wait a minute!" exclaimed Uncle Remus, in response to an expression of intense disappointment in the child's face. "You just wait a minute. The next morning Brer Tarrypin took himself off and wallowed in a mud-hole, smearing himself with mud until he looked exactly like a clod of dirt. Then he crawled off and lay underneath a log where he knew Brer Fox came every morning to exercise himself.

"Brer Tarrypin lay there, and directly there came Brer Fox. By the time he got there, Brer Fox began to jump backward and forward across the log, and Brer Tarrypin got nearer and nearer, until presently he made a grab at Brer Fox and caught him by the foot. They tell me," continued Uncle Remus, rubbing his hands together in token of satisfaction, "they tell me that when Brer Tarrypin once caught hold, it had to thunder before he would let go. All I know is that Brer Tarrypin got Brer Fox by the foot, and he held him there. Brer Fox jumped and he reared, but Brer Tarrypin had got him. Brer Fox shouted:

"'Brer Tarrypin, please let me go!'

"Brer Tarrypin talked down in his throat:

"'Give me my quills!'

"'Do pray let me go and get them.'

"'Give me my quills!'

"And, goodness me! that was all that Brer Fox could get out of Brer Tarrypin. At last, Brer Fox's foot hurt him so much that he was obliged to do something, and he sang out for his wife to fetch the quills. But she was so busy about the house that she didn't hear him. Then he called his son, whose name was Tobe. He shouted and bawled:

"'Tobe! O Tobe! You Tobe!'

"And Tobe answered:

"'What do you want, daddy?'

"'Fetch Brer Tarrypin's quills'

"'What do you say, daddy? Fetch the big tray to get the honey in?'

"'No, you stupid-head! Fetch Brer Tarrypin's quills'

"'What do you say, daddy? Fetch the dipper to catch the minnows in?'

"'No, you fool! Fetch Brer Tarrypin's quills!'

"'What do you say, daddy? Water has been spilt?'

"It went on in this way until after a while Mrs Fox heard the noise, and then she listened. She knew then that her old man was shouting for the quills, so she fetched them out and gave them to Brer Tarrypin, and Brer Tarrypin let go his hold. He let go his hold," Uncle Remus went on, "but a long time after that, when Brer Fox went to pay his calls, he had to go *hoppity-fetchity, hoppity-fetchity*."

The old man folded his hands in his lap, and sat gazing quietly into the lightwood fire. Presently he said:

"I expect Miss Sally is blessing us all by this time, and the first news you know she will get up and have Master John coming down here; and if she does that, then tomorrow morning my breakfast will be cold, and likewise my dinner, and if there's anything I hate it's cold victuals."

Thereupon Uncle Remus arose, shook himself, peered out into the night to discover that the rain had nearly ceased, and then made ready to carry the little boy to his mother. Long before the chickens had crowed for midnight, the child, as well as the old man, had been transported to the land where myths and fables cease to be wonderful—the land of pleasant dreams.

XLII

How Brer Fox failed to get his Grapes

ONE NIGHT the little boy failed to make his appearance at the accustomed hour, and the next morning the intelligence that the child was sick went forth from the 'big house.' Uncle Remus was told that it had been necessary during the night to call in two physicians. When this information was imparted to the old man, there was an expression on his face of awe not unmixed with indignation. He gave vent to the latter:

"There now! Two of them. When that child gets up, if ever he does get up, he certainly will be a shadow. Here am I, going on for eighty years, and I have never taken any of the doctor's stuff yet, except for this bottle of poke-root which old Miss Favers made up for the stiffness in my joints. They'll come and they'll go, and they'll dose the child until he won't look like himself. That's what! And more than that it's very strange to me that old folks can go along and stand whatever comes along and eat their allowance and yet children are struck down. If Miss Sally will turn those doctor-men on to me, I warrant that I'll lick up their physic so that they'll go away astonished."

But no appeal of this nature was made to Uncle Remus. The illness of the little boy was severe, but not fatal. He took his medicine and improved, until finally even the doctors pronounced him convalescent. But he was very weak, and it was a fortnight before he was permitted to leave his bed. He was restless, and yet his term of imprisonment was full of pleasure. Every night after supper Uncle Remus would creep softly into the back piazza, place his hat carefully on the floor, rap gently on the door by way of announcement, and so pass into the nursery. How patient his vigils, how tender his ministrations, only the mother of the little boy knew; how comfortable and refreshing the change from the bed to the strong arms of Uncle Remus, only the little boy could say.

Almost the first manifestation of the child's convalescence was the renewal of his interest in the wonderful adventures of Brer Rabbit, Brer Fox and the other brethren who flourished in that strange past over which this modern Aesop had thrown the veil of fable. "Miss Sally," as Uncle Remus called the little boy's mother, sitting in an adjoining room, heard the youngster pleading for a story, and after a while she heard the old man clear up his throat with a great affectation of formality and begin:

"There was scarcely any point on which old Brer Rabbit and old Brer Fox could agree; let alone that, there was one point between them which was the same as fire and tow, and that was Miss Meadows and the girls. Little as you might expect it, those same creatures were both of them flying around Miss Meadows and the girls. Old Brer Rabbit would go there, and there he would find old Brer Fox sitting up giggling with the girls, and then he would excuse himself and gallop down the big road a bit, and paw up the dust just like that steer which took off your pa's coat-tail last February. And likewise old Brer Fox would saunter in, and find old man Rabbit sitting by the side of the girls, and then he'd go down the road, and grabbing a date-plum bush in his mouth, gnaw the very bark off it. In those days, honey," continued Uncle Remus, responding to a look of perplexity on the child's face, "creatures were worse than they are now. They were that—a lot worse.

"They went on in this way until, by and by, Brer Rabbit began to cast around to see if he couldn't upset some of Brer Fox's arrangements. Once day he was sitting down by the side of the road, working out some arguments which had struck his mind, and fixing up his tricks. Just about the same time he heard a clatter up the long green lane, and there came old Brer Fox—*too-bookity—bookity—bookity-*

book—cantering along like a bay colt. And he was primped up too, looking as slick and shiny as if he had just come out of the store. Old man Rabbit sat there, and when old Brer Fox came galloping along, he got up and hailed him. Brer Fox fetched up, and they passed the time of day with each other most politely; and then Brer Rabbit said that he had some wonderfully good news for Brer Fox. Brer Fox asked him what it was. Then Brer Rabbit scratched his ear with his hind-foot, and said:

"'I was taking a walk the day before yesterday when the first thing that I ran up against was the biggest and fattest bunch of grapes that I ever set eyes on. They were so fat and so big that the juice was just dropping from them, and the bees were swarming after the honey, and Little old Jack Sparrow and all his family connexions were hopping around there dipping in their bills.'

"Right then and there," Uncle Remus went on, "Brer Fox's mouth began to water, and he looked at Brer Rabbit as if he were the best friend that Brer Rabbit had in the round world. He quite forgot all about the girls, and he sidled up to Brer Rabbit and said:

"'Come on, Brer Rabbit, and we'll go down and get those grapes before they are all gone.' And then old Brer Rabbit laughed and responded:

"'I'm hungry myself, Brer Fox, but I'm not hankering after grapes. I shall be in monstrous big luck if I can rush around here somewhere and scrape up a morsel of parsley in time enough to keep the breath in my body. And yet if you go after these grapes, what are Miss Meadows and the girls going to do? I'll warrant that they have got your name in the pot.'

"'As to that,' said old Brer Fox, 'I can drop around and see the ladies afterward.'

"'Well, then, if that's your game,' said old Brer Rabbit, 'I can squat right flat down here on the ground and point out the way to you just as well as if I led you by the hand.' Then Brer Rabbit sort of chewed the cud as if he were searching his memory, and he said:

"'You know that place where you went after sweetgum for Miss Meadows and the girls the other day?'

"Brer Fox declared that he knew that place as well as he knew his own potato-patch.

"'Well, then,' said Brer Rabbit, 'the grapes aren't there. You get to the sweetgum, and then you go up the stream until you come to a little patch of bamboo—but the grapes aren't there. On you go down the hill until you come to another stream, and on that stream there's a dogwood-tree leaning over, and near that dogwood there's a vine, and in that vine there you'll find your grapes. They are that ripe,' said old Brer Rabbit, 'that they look as if they had melted together. I expect you will find them full of insects, but you can take that fine bushy tail of yours, Brer Fox, and brush those insects away.'

"Brer Fox declared that he was much obliged, and then he set out after the grapes in an easy gallop. When he had got well out of sight, and likewise out of hearing, Brer Rabbit took a blade of grass and tickled himself in the ear. Then he shouted and laughed, and laughed and shouted, until he had to lie down so as to get his breath back again.

"Then after some time Brer Rabbit jumped up, and went after Brer Fox, but Brer Fox looked neither to the right nor the left, neither did he look behind: he just kept running along until he came to the sweetgum-tree, and then he turned up by the stream until he came to the bamboo-brier. Then he turned square to the left till he came to the big red oak-root. Then he kept on down the hill until he came to the other stream. There he saw the dogwood. More than that, there near the dogwood he saw the vine, and in that vine was the big bunch of grapes. Sure enough they were all covered with insects.

"Old Brer Rabbit had been pushing along after Brer Fox, but he had to scratch the gravel so as to keep up. At last he came in sight of him, and he lay down among the weeds to watch Brer Fox's motions. Presently Brer Fox crept up the leaning dogwood-tree until he came near the grapes, and then he balanced himself on a limb and gave a swipe with his big bushy tail so as to brush off the insects. But, bless your soul, honey! no sooner had he done that than he squalled so loudly that Miss Meadows declared afterward that she could hear it right down at her house, and down he came—*ker-blim!*"

"What was the matter, Uncle Remus?" the little boy asked.

"Why, honey, that deceitful Brer Rabbit had made a fool of old Brer Fox. Those grapes that were all so fine were neither more nor less than a great big wasps' nest, and the insects were those red wasps—the kind which is full of poison from—end to end. When Brer Fox dropped from the tree the wasps dropped with him, and the way they warmed up old Brer Fox was sinful. They hadn't more than touched him before they had heated him up to boiling-point. Brer Fox ran, and he kicked, he scratched, and he bit; he scrambled, and shouted, and howled; but it looked as if they were getting worse and worse. At one time it seemed as if Brer Fox and his new acquaintances were making toward Brer Rabbit, but they no sooner pointed that way than old Brer Rabbit made a dash, and went sailing through the woods as fast as he could go, and he didn't stop until he came to Miss Meadows's.

"Miss Meadows and the girls asked him whereabouts Brer Fox was, and Brer Rabbit replied that he had gone grape-hunting. Then Miss Meadows said:

"'Law, girls! did you ever hear the like of that? And that too when Brer Fox said that he was coming to dinner. I declare that I have done with Brer Fox, because you can't place any dependence upon these menfolk. Here the dinner has been done a long time, and we have been waiting. But now I have done with Brer Fox.'

"With that, Miss Meadows and the girls asked Brer Rabbit if he would stay to dinner. He pretended that he wanted to be excused, but by and by he took a chair and sat down with them. He took a chair," continued Uncle Remus, "and he hadn't been there long when he looked out and spied Brer Fox going by. What did Brer Rabbit do then but call Miss Meadows and the girls and point him out. As soon as they saw him they set up a great gigglement, because Brer Fox was swelled up so that he was very nearly bursting. His head was swelled up; and right down to his legs, they were swelled up. Miss Meadows said that Brer Fox looked as if he had got all the grapes there were in the neighbourhood, and one of the other girls squealed and said:

"'Law, aren't you ashamed, and here, right in front of Brer Rabbit!'

"And then they held their hands before their faces and giggled just as girls do in these days."

XLIII

BRER FOX PLAYS WITH FIRE

THE NEXT night the little boy had been thoughtful enough to save some of his supper for Uncle Remus, and to this Miss Sally had added on her own account a large piece of fruit-cake. The old man appeared to be highly pleased.

"If there's any kind of cake that I like more than another, it is this kind which has raisins in it. With sick folks now," he continued, holding up the cake and subjecting it to a critical examination, "this hunk would almost last a month, but with a well man like myself it won't last a minute."

And it didn't. It disappeared so suddenly that the little boy laughed aloud, and wanted Uncle Remus to have some more cake; but the latter protested that he didn't come there to get foundered, but merely to see if somebody's strength was strong enough to stand another tale. The little boy said if Uncle Remus meant him he was sure his health was good enough to listen to any number of stories. Whereupon the old man, without any tantalizing preliminaries, began:

"Brer Fox had been fooled so often by Brer Rabbit that he began to look around to see if he could catch up with some of the other creatures, and so, one day while he was going down the big road, whom should he meet but old Brer Tarrypin. Brer Fox licked his chops, and declared to himself that if there was anybody of whom he could get the better it was Brer Tarrypin, and he marched up as if he were going to make sport of him. When he got near enough, Brer Fox hailed him:

"'How do you expect you find yourself this morning, Brer Tarrypin?'

"'Slow, Brer Fox—very slow,' said Brer Tarrypin. 'Day in and day out I'm very slow, and it seems as if I'm getting slower. I'm slow and poorly, Brer Fox—how are you?'

"'Oh, I'm right enough, the same as I always am,' said Brer Fox. 'What makes your eye so red, Brer Tarrypin?'

"'It's all because of the trouble I see, Brer Fox,' said Brer Tarrypin. 'I see trouble and you see none; trouble comes piled up on trouble.'

"'Law, Brer Tarrypin!' said Brer Fox, 'you haven't seen any trouble yet. If you want to see some real trouble, you just ought to go along with me. I'm the man who can show you trouble.'

"'Well then,' said old Brer Tarrypin, 'if you are the man who can show me trouble, then I'm the man who wants a glimpse of it.'

"Then Brer Fox asked Brer Tarrypin if he had seen the Old Boy, and Brer Tarrypin answered that he hadn't seen him, but that he had heard tell of him. With that, Brer Fox declared that the Old Boy was the kind of trouble that he was talking about, and then Brer Tarrypin asked how he was going to see him. Brer Fox; made out the programme, and he told Brer Tarrypin that if he would step up there in the middle of that broomsage field, and squat there a while, it wouldn't be long before he would catch a glimpse of the Old Boy.

"Brer Tarrypin knew that there was something wrong somewhere, yet he was too flat-footed to have any scuffle with Brer Fox, and he said to himself that he would go along and just trust to luck. So he said that if Brer Fox would help him over the fence he believed that he would go up and risk one eye on the Old Boy. Of course Brer Fox helped him across, and no sooner was he really gone than Brer Fox arranged to make him see trouble. He ran to Miss Meadows's house, and pretended that he wanted to borrow a light to light his pipe. He took that chunk of wood and he ran around the field and set the grass afire so that it wasn't long before it seemed as if the whole face of the earth was ablaze."

"Did it burn Brer Tarrypin up?" interrupted the little boy.

"Don't push me, honey; don't make me put the cart before the horse. When old Brer Tarrypin began to wade through the straw, the very first man whom he met was old Brer Rabbit, lying there asleep on the shady side of a tuft. Brer Rabbit was one of these men who sleep with their eyes wide open, and he was awake directly he heard Brer Tarrypin scuffling and scrambling along through the grass. After they had shaken hands and asked about one another's family, it didn't take long for Brer Tarrypin to tell Brer Rabbit what had brought him there, and Brer Rabbit said:

"'It's a born blessing that you met me when you did, because a little more and we both of us would have been roasted whole.'

"This rather terrified Brer Tarrypin, and he said that he wanted to get out from there; but Brer Rabbit said that he would take care of him, so he took Brer Tarrypin to the middle of the field where there was a big hollow stump. On to this stump Brer Rabbit lifted Brer Tarrypin, and then he jumped up himself and crept in the hollow, and, bless your soul, honey, when the fire came snipping and snapping, there they were sat as safe and as snug as you are in bed this minute.

"When the blaze blew over, Brer Tarrypin looked around and saw Brer Fox running up and down the fence as if he were hunting for something. Then Brer Rabbit stuck his head out of the hole and also saw him. Then he shouted like Brer Tarrypin" (here Uncle Remus puckered up his voice, so to say, in a most amusing little squeak):

"'Brer Fox! Brer Fox! O Brer Fox! Run here—we have caught Brer Rabbit!'

"And then Brer Fox jumped on the top rail of the fence and made a spring that landed him away out in the burning grass, which hurt and stung him in the feet so badly that he squealed and rolled, and the more he rolled the worse it burned him. Brer Rabbit and Brer Tarrypin just shouted and laughed. By and by Brer Fox got out, and off he put down the road, limping first on one foot and then on the other."

The little boy laughed, and then there was a long silence—so long, indeed, that Uncle Remus's Miss Sally, sewing in the next room, concluded to investigate it. An exceedingly interesting tableau met her sight. The little child had wandered into the land of dreams with a smile on his face. He lay with one of his little hands buried in both of Uncle Remus's, while the old man himself was fast asleep, with his head back, and his mouth wide open. Miss Sally shook him by the shoulder and held up her finger to prevent him from speaking. He was quiet until she held the lamp for him to get down the back steps, and then she heard him say in an indignantly mortified tone:

"Now, then, Miss Sally will be scolding me for nodding, but instead of that she ought to be glad that I haven't snored so as to alarm the house—let alone that sick baby. That's what!"

XLIV

The Moon in the Mill-Pond

ONE NIGHT when the little boy made his usual visit to Uncle Remus, he found the old man sitting up in his chair fast asleep. The child said nothing. He was prepared to exercise a good deal of patience upon occasion, and the occasion was when he wanted to hear a story. But, in making himself comfortable, he aroused Uncle Remus from his nap.

"I tell you, honey," said the old man, adjusting his spectacles, and laughing rather sheepishly—"I tell you, honey, when I get my head back that way and my eyelids shut and my mouth open and my chin pointing at the rafters, then there's some very queer goings-on in my mind. There are that, as sure as you are sitting here. When I first heard you coming down the path," Uncle Remus continued, rubbing his head thoughtfully, "I was afraid that you might think that I had gone off on a journey to see old man Nod."

This was accompanied by a glance of inquiry, to which the little boy thought it best to respond.

"Well, Uncle Remus," he said, "I did think I heard you snoring when I came in."

"Now you see that!" exclaimed Uncle Remus, in a tone of grieved astonishment; "you see that! A man can't lean himself on his remembrance, but that there is some one to come poking around and declaring that he has gone to sleep. *Shoo!* When you stepped in that door I was right in the middle of some very queer notions—very queer notions. There are no two ways about it; if I were to let you know all the notions that I get in among, folks would have to come and carry me off

The Moon in the Mill Pond

to the place where they put distracted people.

"After supper," Uncle Remus went on, "I heard some flutterments up there in the rafters, and I looked up and there was a bat sailing around. Around and around and around she went—under the rafters, above the rafters—and as she sailed she made a noise as if she were grinding her teeth. Now what that bat was after, I'm blessed if I can tell you, but there she was—around and around, over and under. And by and by out she flipped, and I'll be bound she is still grinding her teeth and going around and around out there, and dodging and flipping just as if the elements were full of rafters and cobwebs.

"When she flipped out I leant my head back, and it wasn't any time before I got mixed up with my notions. That bat's wings were so supple and her will so good that she had done her day's work before you could run to the big house and back. The bat puts me in mind of folks," continued Uncle Remus, settling himself back in his chair, "and folks put me in mind of creatures."

Immediately the little boy was all attention.

"There were times," said the old man, with something like a sigh, "when the creatures would hob-nob together just as if they had never had any fallings-out. Then were the times when old Brer Rabbit would pretend that he was going to give up his bad behaviour, and they would all go around just as if they belonged to the same family connexions.

"At one time after they had been going in shares this way Brer Rabbit began to feel that he was getting fat, and this made him begin to scheme directly. The more peace they had, the worse Brer Rabbit felt, until presently he got restless in his mind. When the sun shone he would go and lie in the grass and kick at the gnats, and nibble at the flower-stalks, and wallow in the sand. One night after supper, while he was roving around, he ran up with old Brer Tarrypin, and after they had shaken hands they sat down by the side of the road and went over old times. They talked and they talked, until by and by Brer Rabbit said things were come to such a pass that he must have some fun. Then

Brer Tarrypin declared that Brer Rabbit was the very man that he had been looking for.

"'Well, then,' said Brer Rabbit, 'we'll just give Brer Fox, and Brer Wolf, and Brer Bear notice, and tomorrow night we'll meet down by the mill-pond and have a little fishing-frolic. I'll do the talking,' said Brer Rabbit, 'and you can sit back and say yea.'

"Brer Tarrypin laughed.

"'If I'm not there,' said he, 'then you may know that the grasshopper has flown away with me.'

"'And you needn't bring any fiddle either,' said Brer Rabbit, 'because there isn't going to be any dancing.'

"With that," continued Uncle Remus, "Brer Rabbit put out for home, and went to bed, while Brer Tarrypin looked around and made his way toward the place so that he could be there at the time appointed.

"The next day Brer Rabbit sent word to the other creatures, and they all made a great to-do, because they hadn't thought of this themselves. Brer Fox declared that he was going after Miss Meadows and Miss Motts and the other girls.

"Sure enough, when the time came, they were all there. Brer Bear brought a hook and line; Brer Wolf also brought a hook and line; Brer Fox brought a dip-net; and Brer Tarrypin, not to be outdone, brought the bait."

"What did Miss Meadows and Miss Motts bring?" the little boy asked.

Uncle Remus dropped his head slightly to one side, and looked over his spectacles at the little boy.

"Miss Meadows and Miss Motts," he continued, "stood back at a safe distance from the edge of the pond and squealed every time that Brer Tarrypin shook the box of bait at them. Brer Bear declared that he was going to fish for mud-cats; Brer Wolf said that he was going to fish for horney-heads; Brer Fox asserted that he was going to fish for perch for the ladies; Brer Tarrypin said that he was going to fish for minnows, and Brer Rabbit winked at Brer Tarrypin and said that he was going to fish for suckers.

"They all got ready, and Brer Rabbit marched up to the pond and prepared to throw the hook in the water, but just then it seemed as if he had seen something. Brer Rabbit dropped his pole and he stood there scratching his head and looking down in the water.

"The girls began to get uneasy when they saw this, and Miss Meadows exclaimed:

"'Goodness me, Brer Rabbit, whatever is the matter in there?'

"Brer Rabbit scratched his head and looked in the water. Miss Meadows held up her petticoats and declared that she was afraid of snakes. Brer Rabbit kept on scratching and looking.

"By and by he drew a long breath, and he said:

"'Ladies and gentlemen, all, we might as well make tracks from this place, because there is no fishing in that pond for any of this crowd.'

"With that, Brer Tarrypin scrambled up to the edge, shook his head and said:

"'To be sure—to be sure! Tut tut tut!' and then he crawled back and looked as if he were thinking very hard.

"'Don't be alarmed, ladies, because we will take care of you, let come what will, let go what must,' said Brer Rabbit. 'Accidents will happen to us all, just as they do to other folks; and there is nothing much the matter, except that the Moon has dropped in the water. If you don't believe me you can look for yourself,' said he.

"With that they all went to the bank and looked in. There, sure enough, lay the Moon, swinging and swaying at the bottom of the pond."

The little boy laughed. He had often seen the reflection of the sky in shallow pools, and the startling depths that seemed to lie at his feet had caused him to draw back with a shudder.

"Brer Fox looked in, and he said, 'Well, well, well!' Brer Wolf looked in, and he said, 'Mighty bad, mighty bad!' Brer Bear looked in, and he said, 'Tum, tum, tum!' The ladies looked in, and Miss Meadows, she screamed, 'Isn't that too bad?' Brer Rabbit, he looked in again, and he said:

"'Ladies and gentlemen, you can all hum and haw, but unless we get that Moon out of the pond, there won't be any fish caught here this night; and if you will ask Brer Tarrypin, he'll tell you the same.'

"Then they asked how they were to get the Moon out of the water, and Brer Tarrypin said they had better leave that to Brer Rabbit. Brer Rabbit shut his eyes, and looked as if he were thinking very hard. Presently he said:

"'The best way out of this difficulty is to send around to old Mr Mud Turtle and borrow his net, and drag the Moon up from there.'

"'I declare to gracious that I'm exceedingly glad you mentioned that,' said Brer Tarrypin.' 'Mr Mud Turtle is such a close relation of mine that I call him Unk Muck, and I'll guarantee that if you send after that net, you won't find Unk Muck disobliging.'

"Well," continued Uncle Remus, after one of his tantalizing pauses, "they sent after that net, and while Brer Rabbit was gone, Brer Tarrypin declared that he had heard time and again that those who find the Moon in the water and fetch it out, will fetch out likewise a pot of money. This made Brer Fox, and Brer Wolf, and Brer Bear feel very pleased, and they said that as Brer Rabbit had been good enough to go after the net, they would do the dragging.

"By the time that Brer Rabbit got back, he saw how the land lay, and he pretended that he wanted to go in after the Moon. He pulled off his coat, and he was starting to take off his waistcoat, but the other creatures declared that they weren't going to let a dry-foot man like Brer Rabbit go in the water. So Brer Fox took hold of one staff of the net, Brer Wolf took hold of the other, and Brer Bear waded behind to lift it across the logs and rocks.

"They made one haul no Moon; another haul—no Moon. Then they got farther out from the bank. The water ran in Brer Fox's ear, and he shook his head; the water ran in Brer Wolf's ear, and he shook his head; the water ran in Brer Bear's ear, and he shook his head. And while they were shaking, they came to the place where the bottom shelved off. Brer Fox stepped off and ducked himself; then Brer Wolf ducked himself; and Brer Bear made a plunge and ducked himself. Goodness me, they kicked and spluttered until it looked as if they were going to splash all the water out of the mill-pond.

"When they came out, the girls were all snickering and giggling, and well they might snicker and giggle, because go where you would there were no worse-looking creatures than they were. Brer Rabbit shouted:

"'I expect you had all better go home, gentlemen, and get some dry clothes, and another time we may have better luck. I have heard that the Moon will take a bite at a hook if you take fools for bait, and I expect that that is the only way to catch her.'

"Brer Fox and Brer Wolf and Brer Bear went off dripping, and Brer Rabbit and Brer Tarrypin, they went home with the girls."

XLV

BRER RABBIT TAKES SOME EXERCISE

ONE NIGHT while the little boy was sitting in Uncle Remus's cabin, waiting for the old man to finish his hoe-cake, and refresh his memory as to the further adventures of Brer Rabbit, his friends and enemies, something dropped upon the top of the house with a noise like the crack of a pistol. The little boy jumped, but Uncle Remus looked up and exclaimed, "Ah-yi!" in a note of triumph.

"What was that, Uncle Remus?" the child asked, after waiting a moment to see what else would happen.

"News from Jack Frost, honey. When that hickory-nut tree out there hears him coming she begins to drop what she has. I'm very glad," he continued, scraping the burnt crust from his hoe cake with an old case-knife, "I'm very glad indeed that hickory-nuts aren't as big and as heavy as grindstones."

He waited a moment to see what effect this queer statement would have upon the child.

"Yes, sir, I'm very glad indeed—that I am. Because if hickory-nuts were as big as grindstones, this old cabin would be leaking long before Christmas."

Just then another hickory-nut dropped upon the roof, and the little boy jumped again. This seemed to amuse Uncle Remus, and he laughed until he was near to choking himself with his smoking hoe-cake.

"You are doing exactly what old Brer Rabbit did, I declare!" the old man cried, as soon as he could get his breath; "exactly for all the world."

The child was immensely flattered, and at once he wanted to know what Brer Rabbit did. Uncle Remus was in such good humour that he needed no coaxing. He pushed his spectacles back on his forehead, wiped his mouth on his sleeve, and began:

"It happened that early one morning, towards the fall of the year, Brer Rabbit was stirring around in the woods after some bergamot so that he could make some hair-grease. The wind was so cold that it made him feel very frisky, and every time that he heard the bushes rustle he looked as if he was frightened. He was going on in this way, hoppity-skippity, when presently he heard Mr Man cutting a tree away off in the woods. He stopped, Brer Rabbit did, and listened first with one ear and then with the other.

"The Man sawed and sawed, and Brer Rabbit listened and listened. By and by, while all this was going on, down came the tree *kubber-lang-bang-blam!* Brer Rabbit jumped just as you jumped, and not only that, he made a break, and leapt up from there as if the dogs were after him."

"Was he frightened, Uncle Remus?" asked the little boy.

"Frightened! Who? *Him?* Shoo! Don't you fret yourself about Brer Rabbit, honey. In those days there was nothing going that could frighten Brer Rabbit. To be sure, he took care of himself, and if you know the man who refuses to take care of himself, I should be very pleased if you would point him out. Indeed I would."

Uncle Remus seemed to boil over with argumentative indignation.

"Well, then," he continued, "Brer Rabbit ran until he began to get hot, and just when he was preparing to squat down and catch his breath, whom should he meet but Brer Coon, going home after sitting up with old Brer Bullfrog. Brer Coon saw him running, and he hailed him:

"'What's your hurry, Brer Rabbit?'

"'I haven't time to stop.'

"'Are your folk sick?'

"'No! I haven't time to stop.'

"'Are you exercising your legs?'

"'No. I haven't time to stop.'

"'Do, pray, Brer Rabbit, tell me the news.'

"'There's a mighty big disturbance back there in the woods. I can't stop.'

"This made Brer Coon feel very frightened, because he was a long way from home. So he just set out, and ran for all he was worth through the woods. He had not gone far when he met Brer Fox.

"'Hullo, Brer Coon, where are you going?'

"'I can't stop.'

"'Are you going to the doctor's?'

"'No. I can't stop.'

"'Do, pray, Brer Coon, tell me the news.'

"'There's a mighty queer disturbance back there in the woods. I can't stop.'

"With that; Brer Fox set out and went faster than the wind. He hadn't gone far before he met Brer Wolf.

"'Hey, Brer Fox! Stop and rest yourself.'

"'I can't stop.'

"'Who is it that wants the doctor?'

"'Nobody. I can't stop.'

"'Do, pray, Brer Fox, tell me the news, good or bad.'

"'There's a mighty curious fuss back there in the woods. I can't stop.'

"With that, Brer Wolf shook himself loose from the face of the earth, and he hadn't gone far when he met Brer Bear. Brer Bear asked the same questions, and Brer Wolf made the same answers, and by and by Brer Bear made a snort and ran off. Goodness me! it wasn't long before the last of the creatures was skedaddling through the woods as if the Old Boy was after him—and all because Brer Rabbit heard Mr Man cutting down the tree.

"They ran and they ran," Uncle Remus went on, "until they came to Brer Tarrypin's house, and then they slowed down because they had

nearly lost their wind. Brer Tarrypin asked them where they were going, and they said that there was a monstrous terrifying racket back
there in the woods. Brer Tarrypin asked what it sounded like. One said
that he didn't know; another said that he didn't know; then they all
said that they didn't know. Then Brer Tarrypin asked who it was that
had heard this monstrous racket. One said that he didn't know; another
said that he didn't know; then they all of them said that they didn't
know. This made old Brer Tarrypin laugh away down in his inside, and
he said:

"'You can all run along if you feel frightened. After I have cooked
my breakfast and washed up the dishes, maybe I'll take down my
parasol and follow after you, if I get wind of any suspicious noise.'

"When the creatures come to make inquiries among themselves as
to who it was that started the news, it went right back to Brer Rabbit,
but, lo and behold! Brer Rabbit wasn't there, and it turned out that
Brer Coon was the man who saw him last. Then they got to laying the
blame on one another, and very soon there would have been a scandalous fight, but old Brer Tarrypin declared that if they wished to
straighten out the matter they had better see Brer Rabbit.

"All the creatures were agreeable, and they set out for Brer Rabbit's
house. When they got there, Brer Rabbit was sitting cross-legged in
the front porch winking his eye at the sun. Brer Bear was the spokes-
man.

"'Why did you make a fool of me, Brer Rabbit?'

"'Make a fool of whom, Brer Bear?'

"'Me, Brer Rabbit, that's who.'

"'This is the first time that I have seen you today, Brer Bear, and you
are more than welcome to that.'

"Then they all asked him the same question and got the same answer. Then Brer Coon put in:

"'Why did you make a fool of me, Brer Rabbit?'

"'How did I make a fool of you, Brer Coon?'

"'You pretended that there was a big racket, Brer Rabbit.'

"'There surely was a big racket, Brer Coon.'

"'What kind of racket, Brer Rabbit?'

"'Ah-ha! You ought to have asked me that first, Brer Coon.'

"'I ask you now, Brer Rabbit.'

"'Mr Man was cutting down a tree, Brer Coon.'

"Of course, this made Brer Coon feel very foolish, and it wasn't long before all the creatures made their bow to Brer Rabbit and slunk off home."

"Brer Rabbit had the best of it all along," said the little boy, after waiting to see if there was a sequel to the story.

"Oh, he did that!" exclaimed Uncle Remus. "Brer Rabbit was a mighty man in those days."

XLVI

WHY BRER BEAR HAS NO TAIL

"I DECLARE, HONEY," Uncle Remus exclaimed one night, as the little boy ran in, "you can't have chewed your food. It hasn't been any time, scarcely, since the supper bell rang. If you go on in this way you will wear yourself out."

"Oh, I wasn't hungry," said the little boy. "I had something before supper, and I wasn't hungry, anyway."

The old man looked keenly at the child, and presently he said:

"The ins and outs of that kind of talk all come to the same point in my mind. You have been misbehaving at the table, and Master John sent you away. While he thinks you are away somewhere sniffling and feeling sad, here you are ranging around as if you had had more supper than the King of Philanders."

Before the little boy could inquire about the King of Philanders he heard his father calling him. He started to go out, but Uncle Remus motioned him back.

"Just sit where you are, honey—just sit still."

Then Uncle Remus went to the door and answered for the child; and a very queer answer it was—one that could be heard half over the plantation:

"Master John, I wish you and Miss Sally would be so good as to let that child alone. He's down here crying his eyes out, and he isn't bothering anybody in the round world."

Uncle Remus stood in the door a moment to see what the reply would be, but he heard none. Thereupon he continued, in the same loud tone:

"I wasn't used to such goings-on in the time of the old Miss, and I'm not going to get used to it now. That I'm not."

Presently 'Tildy, the house-girl, brought the little boy his supper, and the girl was no sooner out of hearing than the child swapped it with Uncle Remus for a roasted yam, and the enjoyment of both seemed to be complete.

"Uncle Remus," said the little boy, after a while, "you know I wasn't crying just now."

"That's so, honey," the old man replied; "but it wouldn't have been long before you would have been, because Master John called out like a man who has a strap in his hand, so what is the difference?"

When they had finished eating, Uncle Remus busied himself in cutting and trimming some soleleather for future use. His knife was so keen, and the leather fell away from it so smoothly and easily, that the little boy wanted to trim some himself. But to this Uncle Remus would not listen.

"It isn't only children who are so conceited as to think that they can do everything that they see other folks do. It's grown folks who ought to know better," said the old man. "That is just the way Brer Bear got his tail broken off *smick-smack-smoove*, and to this day he is the funniest-looking creature that hobbles about on dry ground."

Instantly the little boy forgot all about Uncle Remus's sharp knife.

"It seemed in those days as if Brer Rabbit and Brer Tarrypin had gone into partnership so as to outdo the other creatures. At one time Brer Rabbit paid a call on Brer Tarrypin, but when he got to Brer Tarrypin's house he heard Mrs Tarrypin say that her husband had gone to spend the day with Mr Mud Turtle, who was a near relation of his. Brer Rabbit set out after Brer Tarrypin, and when he reached Mr Mud Turtle's house they all sat up and told tales until twelve o'clock came. Then they had crayfish for dinner, and enjoyed themselves right well. After dinner they went down to Mr Mud Turtle's mill-pond, and when they got there, Mr Mud Turtle and Brer Tarrypin amused themselves with sliding from the top of a big slanting rock into the water.

"You may have seen rocks in the water before now where they get green and slippery," said Uncle Remus.

The little boy had not only seen them, but had found them to be very dangerous to walk upon, and the old man continued:

"Well, then, this rock was very slippery and very slanting. Mr Mud Turtle crawled to the top, let himself go, and went sailing down into the water—*kersplash!* Old Brer Tarrypin followed after, and slid down into the water—*kersplash!* Old Brer Rabbit sat on one side and cheered them on.

"While they were going on in this way, having their fun and enjoying themselves, old Brer Bear came along.

"He heard them laughing and shouting, and he hailed them:

"'Heyo, folks! What's all this? If my eyes don't deceive me, this is Brer Rabbit, Brer Tarrypin, and Uncle Mud Turtle,' said Brer Bear.

"'The same,' said Brer Rabbit; 'and here we are enjoying the day that passes just as if there weren't any hard times.'

"'Well, well, well!' said old Brer Bear, 'a-slipping and a-sliding and making free! And what's the matter with Brer Rabbit that he isn't joining in?' said he.

"Old Brer Rabbit winked at Brer Tarrypin, and Brer Tarrypin nudged Mr Mud Turtle, and then Brer Rabbit up and said:

"'My goodness, Brer Bear! you can't expect a man to slip and slide the whole blessed day, can you? I've had my fun, and now I'm sitting here letting my clothes dry. It's turn and turn about with me and these gentlemen when there's any fun going on.'

"'Maybe Brer Bear would like to join in,' said Brer Tarrypin;

"Brer Rabbit just laughed at this.

"'Shoo! Brer Bear's foot is too big and his tail is too long for him to be able to slide down that rock.'

"This rather put Brer Bear on his mettle, and he said:

"'Maybe they are, and maybe they aren't; yet I'm not afraid to try.'

"With that the others made way for him, and old Brer Bear got up on the rock, he did, and squatted down on his haunches. He curled his tail under him and then started down. At first he went rather slowly, and he grinned as if he liked it; then he went a little faster, and he grinned as if he felt uneasy; then he went faster still, and he grinned as if he were frightened; then he struck the slippery part, and, gentlemen! he swallowed the grin and let out a howl that might have been heard a mile, and he hit the water like a chimney falling.

"You can believe it or not," Uncle Remus continued after a little pause, "but just as surely as you are sitting there, when Brer Bear flew down that rock, he broke his tail off *smack-smack-smoove*, and more than that, when he disappeared up the big road, Brer Rabbit shouted after him:

"'Brer Bear!—O Brer Bear! I have heard that flax-seed poultices are mighty good for sore places!'

"But Brer Bear didn't look back."

XLVII

HOW BRER RABBIT FRIGHTENED HIS NEIGHBOURS

WHEN UNCLE REMUS was in a good humour he turned the most trifling incidents into excuses for amusing the little boy with his stories. One night while he was hunting for a piece of candle on the shelf that took the place of a mantel over the fireplace, he knocked down a tin plate. It fell upon the hearth with a tremendous clatter.

"There now!" exclaimed Uncle Remus. "It's a blessing that that platter has more backbone than the common run of crockery, because it would have gone all to flinderations a long time ago. That platter has dents in it which Miss Sally put there when she was a little bit of a girl. Yet there it is, and this very minute it will hold more food than I have to put in it.

"I warrant," the old man continued, leaning his hand against the chimney and gazing at the little boy reflectively—"I warrant that if the creatures had been here while all that clatterment was going on, they would have left without wishing anybody good-bye. All except Brer Rabbit. Bless your heart, he would have stayed to see the fun, just as he did that other time when he frightened them all so. I expect I have already told you about that."

"When he got the honey on him and rolled in the leaves?"

Uncle Remus thought a moment. "If I make no mistakes in my remembrance, that was the time when he called himself the Will-o'-the-Wisp."

The little boy corroborated Uncle Remus' memory.

"Well, then, this was another time, and it seemed as if he would frighten them right out of the settlement. And it all came about through their wanting to be so smart."

"Who wanted to be smart, Uncle Remus?" asked the child.

"Oh, just those other creatures. They were always laying traps for Brer Rabbit, and getting caught in them themselves. They were always following him day in and day out. I don't deny that some of Brer Rabbit's pranks were very rough, but why didn't they let him alone?"

Naturally the little boy was not prepared to meet these arguments, even had their gravity been less impressive, so he said nothing.

"In those days," Uncle Remus went on, "the creatures were the same as the folks. They had their ups and they had their downs; they had their hard times and they had their soft times. In some seasons the crops would be good, and in some seasons they would be bad. Brer Rabbit fared just like the rest of them. Whatever he made he would spend. One season he planted a fine patch of peanuts, and he declared that if they brought him anything like the money he expected they would, he would go to town and buy whatever his family needed.

"He had no sooner said that than old Mrs Rabbit vowed that it would be a scandal and a shame if he didn't hurry up and get seven tin cups for the children to drink out of, and seven tin plates for them to eat from, and a coffee-pot for the family. Brer Rabbit said that that was exactly what he was going to do, and he declared that he was going to town on the following Wednesday."

Uncle Remus paused, and indulged in a hearty laugh before he resumed:

"Brer Rabbit had only just gone out of the gate when Mrs Rabbit slapped on her bonnet and rushed across to Mrs Mink's house, and she hadn't been there a minute before she told Mrs Mink how that Brer Rabbit had promised to go to town the coming Wednesday and get something for the children. Of course, when Mr Mink came home Mrs Mink declared that she wanted to know why he couldn't buy something for his children as Brer Rabbit was going to do for his, and then they quarrelled just as folks do. After that Mrs Mink carried the news

Why Brer Bear has no tail

How Brer Rabbit frightened his neighbours

to Mrs Fox, and then Brer Fox got hauled over the coals. Mrs Fox told Mrs Wolf, and Mrs Wolf told Mrs Bear; and it wasn't long before everybody in the district knew that Brer Rabbit was going to town the coming Wednesday to get his children something. All the children of the other creatures asked their mothers why their fathers couldn't get *them* something. And so it went on.

"Brer Fox and Brer Wolf and Brer Bear made up their minds that if they were to get even with Brer Rabbit, this was the time. So they made a plan to wait for Brer Rabbit and catch him when he came back from the town. They made all their arrangements and waited for the day.

"Sure enough, when Wednesday came, Brer Rabbit ate his breakfast before the sun rose, and set out for town. He bought for himself a dram, and a plug of tobacco, and a pocket-handkerchief, and for Mrs Rabbit he bought a coffee-pot, and for the children he bought seven tin cups and seven plates. Then towards sundown he started on his journey homeward. He walked along feeling very big at first, but presently he got rather tired and, sitting under a tree, he began to fan himself with one of the plates.

"While he was doing this, a little bit of a woodpecker ran up and down the tree and kept on making ever such a queer noise. After a while Brer Rabbit tried to scare him away with the platter, but this seemed to make the woodpecker more mad than ever, and he rushed out on a branch right over Brer Rabbit's head, and sang:

> "'Pilly-wee, pilly-wee!
> I see what he can't see!
> I see pilly-pee,
> I see what he can't see!'

"He kept on singing this until Brer Rabbit began to look around. He had no sooner done this when he saw marks in the sand where some one had been there before him. He looked a little closer, and then he saw what the woodpecker was driving at. He scratched his head, and then he said to himself:

"'Ah-ha! Here's where Brer Fox has been sitting, and there's the print of his fine bushy tail. Here's where Brer Wolf has been sitting, and there's the print of his fine long tail. Here's where Brer Bear has been squatting on his haunches, and there's the mark where he hasn't got any tail. They have all been here, and I'll be bound that they are hiding in the big gully down there in the hollow.'

"With that, old man Rabbit hid all his goods in the bushes, and then he ran around to see what he could see. Sure enough," continued Uncle Remus, with a curious air of elation, "sure enough, when Brer Rabbit got near the big gully down in the hollow, there they were. Brer Fox was on one side of the road, and Brer Wolf was on the other side, and old Brer Bear was coiled up in the gully taking a nap.

"Brer Rabbit took a peep at them, licked his foot, and put his fur in order, and then he held his hands before his face and laughed as some children do when they think that they are fooling their mothers."

"Not me, Uncle Remus—not me!" exclaimed the little boy promptly.

"Hullo there! don't kick before you are spurred, honey! Brer Rabbit saw them all there, and he grinned, and then he ran to where he had left his goods. When he got there, he danced around and slapped himself on the leg, and made all sorts of curious motions. Then he got to work and turned the coffee-pot upside down on his head. He ran his suspenders through the handles of the cups and slung them across his shoulder. He divided the platters, taking some in one hand and some in the other. After he had got quite ready, he crept to the top of the hill, and, taking a running start, flew down like a hurricane *rickety, rackety, slam-bang!*"

The little boy clapped his hands enthusiastically.

"Bless your soul, those creatures had never heard a noise like that before, and they had never seen a man who looked like Brer Rabbit, with the coffee-pot on his head, the cups rattling on the end of the suspenders, and the platters a-waving and a-shining in the air.

"Now, mind you, old Brer Bear was lying up in the gully taking a nap, and the noise frightened him so much that he made a dash and ran over Brer Fox. He rushed out in the road, and when he saw the sight he ran over Brer Wolf. With their scrambling and their scuffling, Brer Rabbit got right on them before they could get away. He shouted:

"'Give me room! Turn me loose! I'm old man Spewter-splutter with long claws, and scales on my back! I'm snaggle-toothed and double-jointed! Give me room!'

"Every time he would give a whoop, he would rattle the cups and slap the platters together—*rickety, rackety, slam-bang!* And I tell you that when those creatures got their limbs together they split the wind, that they did. Old Brer Bear struck a stump that stood in the way, and I am not going to tell you how he tore it up, because you wouldn't believe me; but next morning Brer Rabbit and his children went back there and got enough splinters to last them for lighting fires for all the winter. Yes, sir! That's as sure as I am sitting here by this hearth."

XLVIII

Mr Man has some Meat

THE LITTLE BOY sat watching Uncle Remus sharpen his shoe-knife. The old man's head moved in sympathy with his hands, and he mumbled fragments of a song. Occasionally he would feel the edge of the blade with his thumb, and then begin to sharpen it again. The comical appearance of the venerable old man finally had its effect upon the child, for suddenly he broke into a hearty peal of laughter; whereupon Uncle Remus stopped shaking his head and singing his mumbled song, and assumed a very dignified attitude. Then he drew a long deep breath, and said:

"When folks get old and stricken with the palsy, they must expect to be laughed at. Goodness knows, I have been used to that ever since my whiskers began to bleach."

"Why, I wasn't laughing at you, Uncle Remus; I declare I wasn't," cried the little boy. "I thought maybe you might be moving your head as Brer Rabbit was when he was trying to cut his meat."

Uncle Remus's seriousness was immediately driven away by a broad and appreciative grin.

"Now, that's the way to talk, honey, and I'll be bound that you are not far wrong, either. For though they tell you that Brer Rabbit makes his living by nibbling at grass and greens, it wasn't so in those days, because I can remember the time when Brer Rabbit took and ate some meat."

The little boy had learned that it was best not to make any display of impatience, and so he waited quietly while Uncle Remus busied himself with arranging the tools on his shoe-bench. Presently the old man began:

"It so happened that one day Brer Rabbit met Brer Fox, and when they had inquired after each other's health, they found that they were both very poorly. Brer Fox declared that he was terribly hungry, and Brer Rabbit replied that he had a great hankering after something to eat himself. By and by they looked up the big road and saw Mr Man coming along with a great hunk of beef under his arm. Brer Fox said that he would like very well to get a taste of that beef, and Brer Rabbit said that the sight of that delicious meat all lined with fat was enough to make a body distracted.

"Mr Man came and came along. Brer Rabbit and Brer Fox looked and looked at him. They blinked their eyes, and their mouths began to water. Then Brer Rabbit declared that he must get some of that meat, somehow. Brer Fox replied that to him it looked very far off. Then Brer Rabbit told Brer Fox to follow along after him in hailing distance, and with that he set out, and it wasn't long before he caught up to Mr Man.

"They passed the time of day, and then they went jogging along the road just as if they were going upon a journey. Brer Rabbit kept on sniffing the air. Mr Man asked him if he had a bad cold, to which Brer Rabbit replied that he smelt something which wasn't exactly like ripe peaches. Presently Brer Rabbit began to hold his nose, and after a while he sang out:

"'Goodness gracious, Mr Man! it's that meat of yours. *Phew!* Whereabouts did you pick it up?'

"This made Mr Man feel rather ashamed of himself, and, to make matters worse, there came a great big blue-bottle fly a-zooning around. Brer Rabbit got away to the side of the road, and kept on holding his nose. Mr Man looked a little sheepish, and they hadn't gone far before he put the meat down on the side of the road, and asked Brer Rabbit what they could do about it. Brer Rabbit declared:

"'I have heard it said before now that if you drag a piece of meat through the dust it will fetch back its freshness. I am not a superstitious man myself, and I haven't had any experience of such things, though the folks who have told me say that they have tried it. But I do know this. It can't do any harm, because the grit which gets on the meat can be washed off.'

"'I haven't got any string,' said Mr Man.

"Brer Rabbit laughed heartily, but still he held his nose.

"'By the time you have lived in the bushes as long as I have, you won't want for string,' said Brer Rabbit.

"With that Brer Rabbit ran off, and he hadn't been gone long before he came hopping back with a whole bundle of bamboo vines all tied together. Mr Man then said:

"'That line is very long.'

"Brer Rabbit declared:

"'To be sure, you want the wind to get between you and that meat.'

"Then Mr Man tied the bamboo line to the meat, while Brer Rabbit broke off a date-plum bush and said that he would stay behind and keep the flies off. So Mr Man went in front and dragged the meat, while Brer Rabbit stayed behind and took care of it."

Here Uncle Remus was compelled to pause and laugh before he could proceed with the story.

"And he did take care of it, man—that he did. He got a rock, and while Mr Man went along without looking back, he undid the meat and tied the rock to the bamboo line, and when Brer Fox followed on, sure enough, there lay the meat. Mr Man dragged the rock, and Brer Rabbit kept the flies off, until they had gone on a good way. Then when Mr Man looked around, where was old man Rabbit?

"Bless your heart, Brer Rabbit had gone back and joined Brer Fox; and he was just in time, because a little more and Brer Fox would have been out of sight and hearing. And so that was the way that Brer Rabbit got Mr Man's meat."

The little boy reflected a little, and then said:

"Uncle Remus, wasn't that stealing?"

"Well, I'll tell you about that, honey," responded the old man, with the air of one who is willing to compromise. "In those days the creatures were obliged to look out for themselves, more especially those who had neither horns nor hoofs. Brer Rabbit had neither horn nor hoof, and so he had to be his own lawyer."

Just then the little boy heard his father's carriage rattling down the avenue, and he ran out into the darkness to meet it. After he was gone, Uncle Remus sat a long time rubbing his hands and looking serious. Finally he leaned back in his chair, and exclaimed:

"That little chap is getting too much for old Remus—that he is."

XLIX

How Brer Rabbit got the Meat

WHEN THE little boy next visited Uncle Remus the cabin was dark and empty and the door shut. The old man was gone. He was absent for several nights, but at last one night the little boy saw a welcome light in the cabin, and he made haste to pay Uncle Remus a visit. He was full of questions:

"Goodness, Uncle Remus! where in the world have you been? I thought you were gone for good. Mamma said she reckoned the treatment here didn't suit you, and you had gone off to get some of your town friends to hire you."

"Did Miss Sally tell you that, honey? Well, if she isn't the most remarkable woman this side of kingdom come, you can just shoot me. Miss Sally wrote me a pass with her own hands so that I could go and see some of my folks down there in the Ashbank settlement. Your mammy is a queer woman, surely!

"And yet, what's the good of my staying here? The other night I hadn't got more than well started before you were up and gone, and I haven't seen hair nor hide of you since. When I saw you do that, I said to myself that it was about time for old man Remus to pack up his belongings and find company somewhere else."

"Well, Uncle Remus," exclaimed the little boy, ill a tone of expostulation, "didn't Brer Fox get the meat, and wasn't that the end of the story?"

Uncle Remus started to laugh, but he changed his mind so suddenly that the little boy was convulsed. The old man groaned and looked at the rafters with a curious air of disinterestedness. After a while he went on with great seriousness:

"I don't know what kind of idea folks have got about Brer Rabbit, anyhow, that I don't. Suppose you make plans so that some other chap can get a big hunk of goodies, are you going to sit by and see him eat them all?"

"What kind of goodies, Uncle Remus?"

"The kind of goodies that these town folks keep. Mint drops and raisins, and sweet-stuff such as Miss Sally keeps under lock and key. Well, then, if you had some of that, and maybe some other kind of goody which I wish was here at this very minute, are you going to sit quiet up there in that chair and let another chap run off with it? That you are not—that you are not!"

"Oh, I know!" exclaimed the little boy. "Brer Rabbit went back and made Brer Fox give him his part of the meat."

"Just as I tell you, honey; there was no man among the creatures who could stand on his feet and work his mind quickly as Brer Rabbit could. He tied the rock on the string instead of the meat, and he went along after it until Mr Man turned a bend in the road. Then Brer Rabbit just ran off from there—*terbuckity-buckity, buck-buck-buckity!* and it wasn't long before he caught up to Brer Fox. They took the meat and carried it away off in the woods, and laid it down on a clean place on the ground.

"They laid it down, they did," continued Uncle Remus, drawing his chair up closer to the little boy, "and then Brer Fox said that they had better sample it. Brer Rabbit agreed. With that, Brer Fox gnawed off a hunk, shut both his eyes, and chawed and chawed, and tasted and tasted, and chawed and tasted. Brer Rabbit watched him, but Brer Fox kept both eyes shut, and chawed and tasted, and tasted and chawed."

Uncle Remus not only furnished a pantomime accompaniment to this recital by shutting his eyes and pretending to taste, but he lowered his voice to a pitch of tragical significance in reporting the dialogue that ensued:

"Then Brer Fox smacked his lips and, looking at the meat more closely, declared:

"'Brer Rabbit, *it's lamb!*'

"'No, Brer Fox, *surely not!*'

"'Brer Rabbit, *it's lamb!*'

"'Brer Fox, *oh! surely not!*'

"Then Brer Rabbit gnawed off a hunk, and, shutting both eyes, chawed and tasted, and tasted and chawed. Then he smacked his lips, and said:

"'Brer Fox, *it's pork!*'

"'Brer Rabbit, you are fooling me!'

"'Brer Fox, I vow *it's pork!*'

"'Brer Rabbit, it just *can't be!*'

"'Brer Fox, it *surely is!*'

"They tasted and disputed, and they disputed and they tasted. After a while, Brer Rabbit made as if he wanted some water, and he rushed off in the bushes. Soon back he came wiping his mouth and clearing his throat. Then Brer Fox wanted some water as well:

"'Brer Rabbit, where did you find that spring?'

"'Across the road, and down the hill, and up the big gully.'

"Brer Fox leapt off, and after he was gone, Brer Rabbit touched his ear with his hind-foot as if he was flipping him good-bye. Brer Fox crossed the road, and rushed down the hill, and yet he couldn't find any big gully. He kept on until he found the big gully, and yet he couldn't find any spring.

"While all this was going on, Brer Rabbit scraped a hole in the ground, and in that hole he hid the meat. After he had quite hidden it, he cut a long keen hickory stick. A long while after, when he heard Brer Fox coming back, he got in a clump of bushes, and with that hickory let out at a sapling. Every time that he hit the sapling he would squall just as if the patrollers had him:

"*Pow, pow!* 'Oh, pray, Mr Man!'—*Pow, pow!* 'Oh, pray, Mr Man!'—*Chippy-row, pow!* 'Oh! lordy, Mr Man! Brer Fox took your meat!'—*Pow!* 'Oh, pray, Mr Man! Brer Fox took your meat!'"

Every time Uncle Remus said "*Pow!*" he struck himself in the palm of his hand with a shoe-sole by way of illustration.

"Of course," he went on, "when Brer Fox heard this kind of doings, he stopped and listened, and every time that he heard the hickory come down *pow!* he grinned, and said to himself, 'Ah-ha! you fooled me about the water! Ah-ha! you fooled me about the water!'

"After a time the noise died down, and it seemed as if Mr Man was dragging Brer Rabbit off. This made Brer Fox feel rather frightened. By and by Brer Rabbit shouted back:

"'Run, Brer Fox, run! Mr Man says he is going to carry that meat up the road to where his son is, and then he is coming back after you. Run, Brer Fox, run!'

"And I tell you," said Uncle Remus, leaning back in his chair and laughing to see the little boy laugh, "I tell you that Brer Fox made himself very scarce in that neighbourhood!"

L

BRER WOLF SAYS GRACE

THE LITTLE BOY'S mother, thinking that he had spent too much of his time with Uncle Remus, would not allow him to visit the old man for a time. The child amused himself as best he could for several nights, but his playthings and picture-books finally lost their interest. He cried so hard to be allowed to go to see Uncle Remus, however, that his mother placed him under the charge of Aunt Tempy, a woman of large authority on the place, who stood next to Uncle Remus in the confidence of her mistress.

"Why, goodness me!" exclaimed Uncle Remus, as Aunt Tempy went in with the little boy. "How are you, Sis Tempy? The rainy weather can't be so very far off when you pay a visit to this house. If I had known you were coming I would have bustled around and brushed the cobwebs out of the corners."

"Don't mind me, Brer Remus. There's luck in the house where the cobwebs hang low. I was just passing and Miss Sally asked me if I would come as far with that child."

"Well, he hasn't been down here for so long that I suppose I ought to tell him a story. It has just come into my mind that there was one time when Brer Wolf caught Brer Rabbit, and I have never yet told you about it."

"Brer Wolf caught Brer Rabbit, Uncle Remus?" exclaimed the little boy incredulously.

"Yes, sir! that's the long and the short of it, for certain," responded the old man with emphasis, "and I shall be very glad if Sis Tempy here will excuse me while I tell you the tale."

"Bless your soul, Brer Remus, don't pay any attention to me," said Aunt Tempy, folding her fat arms. "I'm as bad as the children about those old tales. I could just sit here and listen to them the whole of the night, and a good part of the day. Indeed I could."

"Well, then," said Uncle Remus, "we will just huddle up here and see what came of Brer Rabbit when old Brer Wolf caught him. In those days the creatures were always running around after the girls. And it was none of this 'How-do-you-do-ma'am-I-expect-I-had-better-be-going,' either. They would go after breakfast and stay till after supper. Brer Rabbit took a fancy for Miss Motts, and one morning he smartened himself up and set out to call on her. When he got to where Miss Motts lived he found that she was out.

"Some folks would have sat down and waited until she came back; other folks would have gone away again; but old Brer Rabbit was not the man to be outdone. He went in the kitchen and lit his cigar, then he set out to pay a call on Miss Meadows and the girls.

"When he got there, lo and behold! there was Miss Motts. So Brer Rabbit went in and behaved just like a man from town. They talked and they laughed; they laughed and they giggled. After a time, when it was getting on toward night, Brer Rabbit declared that he had better be going. The ladies all asked him to stay to supper because he was such lively company, but Brer Rabbit was afraid that one or other of the creatures would be waiting to catch him, so he paid his respects and set out for home.

"He hadn't gone far when he came across a basket by the side of the big road. He looked up the road; there was nobody there. He looked down the road, there was nobody there. He looked before, he looked behind, he looked all around; nobody was in sight. He listened, and listened; he couldn't hear anything. He waited and waited; nobody came.

"Then Brer Rabbit went and peeped in the basket: it seemed to be half full of green-stuff. He put his hand in and got some of it and put it in his mouth. Then he shut his eyes as if he was thinking hard about something. After a while he said to himself, 'It looks like sparrow-grass, it feels like sparrow-grass, it tastes like sparrow-grass, and I'm blest if it isn't sparrow-grass.'

"With that Brer Rabbit jumped up, cracked his heels together, and gave one leap, landing right in the basket in the middle of the sparrow-grass. That was where he missed his footing," continued Uncle Remus, thoughtfully rubbing his beard, "because when he jumped in among the sparrow-grass, right then and there he jumped in with old Brer Wolf, who was curled up at the bottom.

"The minute Brer Wolf grabbed him Brer Rabbit knew that his was a gone case; yet he sang out:

"'I was just trying to frighten you, Brer Wolf, I was just trying to frighten you. I knew you were in there, Brer Wolf. I knew you by the smell!'

"Old Brer Wolf grinned and, licking his lips, said:

"'I'm very glad you knew me, Brer Rabbit, because I knew you the minute you dropped in on me. I told Brer Fox yesterday that I was going to take a nap by the side of the road, and I was sure that you would come along and wake me up. And, sure enough, you came, and here you are.'

"When Brer Rabbit heard this," said Uncle Remus, "he began to get terribly frightened, and he begged Brer Wolf please to let him off. But this only made Brer Wolf grin more than ever, and his teeth looked so long and shone so white that Brer Rabbit kept quiet and stayed still. He was so afraid that his breath came quickly, and his heart went pit-a-pat. He then made a noise as if he were going to cry:

"'Where are you going to take me, Brer Wolf?'

"'Down by the stream, Brer Rabbit.'

"'What are you going down there for, Brer Wolf?'

"'To get some water to clean you after I have skinned you, Brer Rabbit.'

"'Please, sir, let me go, Brer Wolf.'

"'When you talk like that you make me laugh, Brer Rabbit.'

"'The sparrow-grass has made me feel sick, Brer Wolf.'

"'You will be more sick than that before I have done with you, Brer Rabbit.'

"'Where I come from, they are afraid to eat sick folks, Brer Wolf.'

"They went on in this way," continued Uncle Remus, "until they got to the stream. Brer Rabbit begged and cried, and cried and begged, while Brer Wolf refused and grinned, and grinned and refused. When they reached the stream, Brer Wolf put Brer Rabbit on the ground and held him there, while he thought how he could make away with him. He thought and thought, and while he was thinking, Brer Rabbit did some thinking for himself.

"Then, when it seemed as if Brer Wolf had made all his arrangements, Brer Rabbit pretended to be crying worse and worse; he fairly blubbered."

Uncle Remus gave a ludicrous imitation of Brer Rabbit's wailings:

"'Ber-ber-Brer Wooly-ooly-oolf! Are you going—are you going to kill me now-ow-ow?'

"'That I am, Brer Rabbit; that I am.'

"'Well, if I must be killed, Brer Wooly-ooly-oolf, I want to be killed properly; and if I must be eaten, I want to be eaten properly, too!'

"'What do you mean, Brer Rabbit?'

"'I want you to show your politeness, Brer Wooly-ooly-oolf!'

"'How am I to do that, Brer Rabbit?'

"'I want you to say grace, Brer Wolf, and say it quickly, because I am getting very weak.'

"'How must I say grace, Brer Rabbit?'

"'Fold your hands under your chin, Brer Wolf, and shut your eyes, and say: "Bless us and bind us and put us in a crack where the Old Boy can't find us." Say it quickly, Brer Wolf, because I am failing fast.'

"So Brer Wolf put up his hands, shut his eyes, and said, 'Bless us and bind us'; but he didn't get any farther, because at the very minute he took up his hands, Brer Rabbit gave a wriggle, got on to his feet, and just left a blue streak behind him."

"Oh, I knew Brer Rabbit would get away," the little boy declared.

"That's right, honey," said Uncle Remus. "You depend upon Brer Rabbit and you won't be far out of the way."

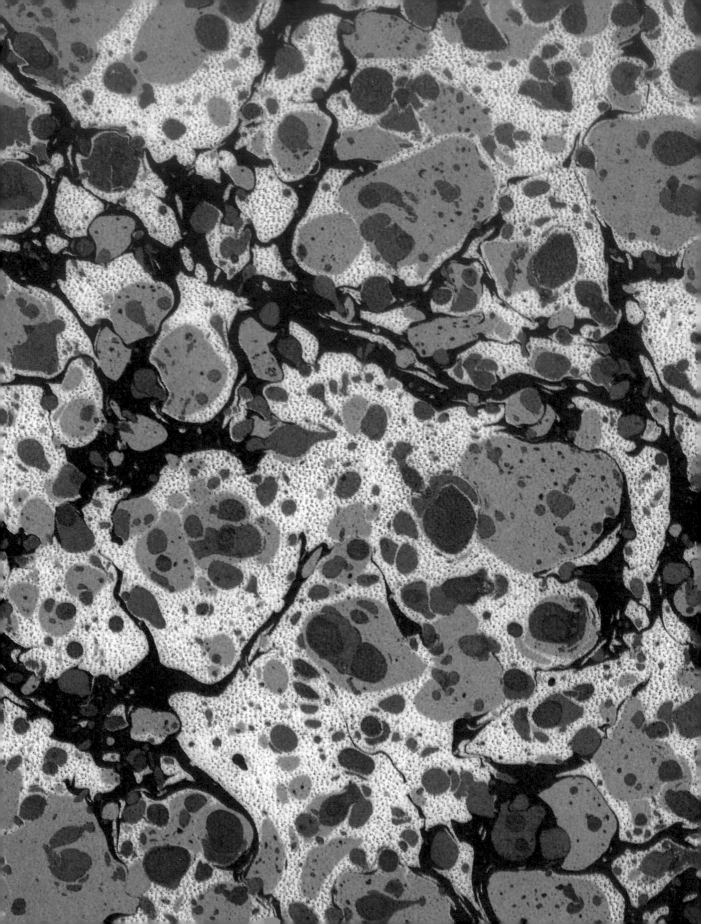